LINGER

Edward Fallon

#5

The
Death
of
Dreams

BRAUN HAUS MEDIA, LLC

This is a work of fiction. All of the characters, organizations, and events portrayed in this novel are either products of the author's imagination or are used fictitiously.

LINGER #5 The Death of Dreams
Copyright © 2015 by Braun Haus Media, LLC
All rights reserved.

Cover design by Braun Haus Media, LLC
Photo Credits:
Angry Teen Girl © Alexander Trinitatov / Dollar Photo Club

*The publisher wishes to acknowledge
and thank Rob Cornell
for his contribution to this work*

Sign up for the
Braun Haus Media, LLC Newsletter
and get a free ebook.

Yes, that's right.
A free full-length supernatural thriller
from our growing library of books.

See BraunHausMedia.com for details

Other books in the *Linger* series available for purchase now

LINGER 5

The Death of Dreams

PART ONE

"Death gives us sleep, eternal youth, and immortality."

~Jean Paul

1

THE COLD SEEPED DOWN INTO Kate Messenger's bones.

Despite the parka she had picked up in Toledo, and the wool-lined gloves, and the hot-pink knit cap (the only one left at a small town department store that fit her), the cold had set in and refused to let go. She had the Rambler's heater cranked to the max—despite Weston's gripes—and would occasionally press her gloved hands against the dash vent. Still, no good. Kate's California blood wasn't meant for this kind of climate.

The Rambler was an old '64 station wagon her companion, Noah Weston, had inherited from his wife after her murder. He understandably clung to it, but his devotion to the vehicle outstretched the wagon's dedication to him. The heater worked, but an occasional rattle from within worried Kate that it might not stand up against the Midwestern winter.

Weston sat behind the wheel. He wore a turtleneck knit

with snowflakes and reindeer—the least offensive sweater he could find in a town where such attire was apparently fashionable.

Weston had shrugged off his own parka and had tossed it in the backseat after only ten minutes with the heater on. He obviously had a higher tolerance for freezing damn cold.

The view outside added to the chill inside of Kate.

The sky was sheet metal gray. On either side of the two-lane highway they'd been traveling on for over an hour now, farmland stretched to the far horizon, ending at black walls of naked maples and oaks. The stubs of chopped cornstalks peeked above a layer of snow, curled and brown. An occasional line of pine trees separated some of the farms. And the only other thing breaking up the barren plains of snow were the occasional farmhouses with sagging porches, frosted windows, and icicles hanging from the eaves.

Kate folded her arms across her chest and hunched into her parka.

The *whoosh* of hot air out of the vents carried with it a hot plastic smell that made Kate feel queasy. But she would happily suffer a little car sickness in place of the frost under her skin.

"It isn't that bad," Weston said. He stared ahead, his eyes full of that seemingly permanent solemnity that made Kate think of a priest for some reason. If not for the fact that he'd lost all faith in God, she could picture him taking confessions and assigning hail Marys to guilty sinners.

"Oh, it's bad. Forget fire and brimstone. If there's a hell, it's made of ice."

Weston snorted and shook his head. Then fell back to silence.

They had sat through a lot of silence on this leg of their trip, and it had grown all the thicker when they crossed the border into Michigan.

All because of the pull.

Kate twisted in her seat to peek in on Christopher in the back. He rocked gently as he often did, his hands flat on his lap as if holding down his legs. He had refused a parka of his own, content to wear a gray hoodie with the hood up. The cold didn't appear to bother him at all.

His blind gaze seemed to stare *through* the air, as if he peered into some other world, a place where his blindness didn't matter. And Kate could believe it, from what she had experienced since joining the man and the boy on their cross-country quest. His silence, of course, was something she had grown accustomed to. The man responsible for tearing apart all three of their lives—and, in turn, bringing them together—had cut out the boy's tongue and left him for dead.

Christopher had other ways of communicating with them. But after the three of them first felt the pull, he hadn't offered any communication at all, lost in what Weston referred to as the haze.

That had been two days ago.

"Are you okay, Christopher?" Kate asked.

He continued to rock. Said nothing.

She turned forward. A concrete silo poked above a rise in the road, the top missing and the concrete crumbling. Kate had seen several in similar condition, as if they'd become obsolete but were so wedded to the landscape no one dared tear them down.

Kate felt a tingle at the back of her brain accompanied by a dull pain like what you'd get from eating ice cream too fast, only in the wrong part of her head. The tingle was nothing new. She'd almost grown used to it over the last couple days. The pain, on the other hand, was something fresh. And she thought she knew where it came from.

"We're close."

Weston nodded. "The ping is louder."

He had taken to referring to the pull in sonar terms. The closer they got to whatever drew them to this winter wasteland, the louder the ping. Kate envisioned it more as an invisible rope fastened to her head, tugging gently, but never too hard. Until now. Maybe she felt the pain because that tug had turned into a firm yank.

They cleared the rise before the silo and passed a nearby barn with a sunken roof and a car-sized hole in the faded red planks of one side. After another fifty yards they came upon a green roadside sign with white print welcoming them to Coolidge Township. Another rise hid what lay beyond.

Weston slowed.

"What's wrong?" Kate asked, but sensed she knew.

"It's up ahead."

Yeah. Kate felt it too. After nearly thirty hours of travel in a winding, convoluted route, they had arrived.

It was usually Christopher who guided them to their next destination.

Not this time.

Whatever *this* was, it spoke directly to all three of them.

I feel something... different, Christopher had said to her with his thoughts Tuesday morning. They were having breakfast in a Biloxi diner—Mississippi weather was *so* much nicer than this Midwestern tundra.

Weston had winced down at his plate as if his sunny-side up eggs were a little too sunny. "Are *you* doing this?" he'd asked Christopher.

Kate, feeling that tingle, had scratched the back of her head, but couldn't reach the itch inside. "No," she said. "He —"

Different!

Weston had jerked back, same as Kate, both of them hearing Christopher's psychic shout, which had been his last communication with them.

Now, Weston brought the Rambler to a full stop just before the rise. He glanced at Kate, face tight. "What are we in for here?"

"I have no idea."

He turned the knob on the heater, cutting the persistent sigh from the vents. The idling motor rumbled, but the car was otherwise quiet. "We want to see what's on the other side of that rise? Or do we want to turn around?"

Kate was glad Weston sounded as creeped out by this new pull thing as she was. It felt wrong. Not the way their mission to find the Beast was supposed to work. In fact, Kate suspected the Beast had nothing to do with why they felt drawn to Southeast Michigan, to Coolidge Township, and to whatever lay beyond the rise.

We can't turn around.

Kate gasped, startled by the sudden touch of Christopher's mind after such a long silence. She turned in her seat to look back at him. "Do you know why we're here?"

Even though he was blind, he looked at her, and she felt as if he could see her.

No.

Kate waited for more, but Christopher leaned back, and returned his hands to his lap. His gaze turned inward.

She looked at Weston and raised an eyebrow. "I guess we can't turn around."

Weston sighed. "Of course we can't." He eased his foot off the brake and the Rambler rolled forward. "Let's see what we've got in store."

As they crested the rise, the hair on the back of Kate's

neck stood on end. But the pain and the tingling in her head stopped, as if the line reeling her in had snapped.

Which made sense. She didn't need to be pulled anymore.

They had arrived.

2

NOAH WESTON WASN'T SURE WHAT he had expected to find as the Rambler crested the rise. A vicious dragon? An active volcano? Zombies? Nothing so dramatic. But he sure as hell hadn't expected something so... mundane.

About a hundred yards beyond the rise, a small village sat under a dust of snow. The village had a short main street and shops with old brick facades lined along either side. A blinking yellow traffic light hung above the only visible intersection.

Beyond the village, the two-lane road they had traveled for nearly two hours now continued away to the horizon, passing the only building outside the central cluster that formed the village's downtown—if you could call it that: a grocery store, its windows boarded, its asphalt parking lot cracked and crumbling, with a marquee out front announcing the last sale of the store's life: P RK TEND RL N $ 1.49/ P U D.

On either side of the main street, behind the shops, around thirty or forty houses sat in a rough grid. Most of them looked as if they'd been built in the late fifties. They huddled close together, and every other house seemed to have fallen into decay, wood siding rotten and peeling, untouched snow hiding their driveways and sidewalks out front.

But the other houses had shoveled drives, fresh siding painted with vibrant colors, and gutters that hadn't bent and drooped under years of neglect.

The village had a gas station too, tucked in one corner of the intersection.

The only thing ominous about this place was its silence. The snow and cold seemed to have driven all the residents indoors, leaving their small town looking vacant. If not for lights in the windows of the shops and some of the homes, Weston might have mistaken it for a ghost town with wisps of snow blowing in the wind instead of tumbleweeds.

He had stopped again on top of the rise.

Kate leaned toward the windshield, brow furrowed. "It doesn't look evil," she said. "Just... tiny."

"It's probably the closest thing to a city in the township. Everything else is farmland."

Weston glanced in the rearview at Christopher. He wished the boy would give them some sort of direction, maybe connect with Weston to inspire a sketch of a face, a building, a stretch of sidewalk. Anything. But laying this all on Christopher wasn't fair. The need to come to this place hadn't only come from the boy, it had come from all three of them.

And even though the little village before them looked innocent enough, that strange fact left Weston wary about this place.

"Where do we go next?" Kate asked.

Weston shrugged. "I'm not feeling anything anymore."

"Neither am I."

They both turned to Christopher. It was funny how much they depended on the boy now. Sometimes it felt as if he were the adult in the driver's seat and Weston and Kate were simply along for the ride.

But their driver seemed as lost as his passengers.

Christopher had gone incredibly still, as if frozen from the cold, even though Kate had made sure the Rambler doubled as a broiler. Weston tried to reach out to the boy with his mind. No luck. Just a blank wall he couldn't push through.

Weston sighed and faced forward. A small flurry had begun, only a sparse fall of flakes. Those snowflakes that landed on the windshield melted instantly. "It looks like there's a restaurant in town. I could use a sandwich and a cup of coffee." He wasn't really hungry, but they hadn't stopped to eat for nearly ten hours. His body needed fuel whether he wanted it or not. And coffee, hopefully, would clear the sleepiness out of his eyes.

"Why not?" Kate said.

Weston eased off the brake and they rolled down the rise and into town.

3

IT LOOKED AS IF HALF THE town had come in for a late lunch.

The restaurant sported an open floor plan with a cashier's counter by the entrance and a kitchen at the back. The plain tile floors and the tables with straight metal legs and brown fiberboard tops made the place look more like a high school cafeteria than a small town diner. No lunch counter or jukebox.

The wait staff wore jeans and black T-shirts with "Sammy's" printed in white cursive on the back—apparently the name of the restaurant. Kate hadn't seen a sign outside, only the plate-glass window that stretched the length of the building and a whiteboard in the window with the date and the daily special written in red and green marker.

Kate, Weston, and Christopher stood just inside the front door, a light dust of snow on their shoulders. In the time it had taken to drive into town and park the Rambler at the curb across the street, the flurry had turned into a snowfall steady enough to powder them on their way from the car to the restaurant.

Only three waitresses scrambled back and forth between the kitchen and the forty-odd patrons crowding the place. Most of the tables lined the walls. The persistent hum of chatter never stalled.

The smell of fried food hung thick in the air.

Kate's stomach grumbled. She hadn't known she was hungry until now.

In the center of the room, a long table that could seat at least a dozen, like a Thanksgiving dinner table, dominated the space. Nearly every chair at the table was taken, all of them by men ranging from their early twenties to one who looked close to ninety. They all wore similar clothes, like uniforms. Denim coveralls over flannel shirts.

Except for the man at the head of the table.

He wore a dress shirt and skinny black tie. He looked to be in his mid-fifties, though his curly hair had already gone a stark white, like a cloud settled onto his head. As he chatted with the men on his end of the table, he laughed frequently, a full, hearty laugh that boomed through all the other noise in the restaurant. The laugh did not jive with his thin frame. It sounded like it should have come from a jolly fat man. Like Santa Claus.

Kate and her companions stood there a good five minutes before one of the waitresses, barely in her twenties, broke free from the madness long enough to find them a table.

Weston sat across from Kate with Christopher at his side. He looked around. "I think we found Coolidge Township's hot spot."

Kate nodded toward the center table. "What do you think of the king's table and his coveralled knights?"

Weston smirked. "Farmers of the rectangular table?"

"It's weird, huh?"

He shrugged. "Farmers have to socialize somewhere after working all day alone."

"I guess."

Kate pulled out a pair of laminated menus tucked behind a ketchup bottle and a pair of salt and pepper shakers. She passed one over to Weston, opened hers, and saw no surprises. Standard fare. Burgers. Omelets. Chicken fingers. Chicken soup.

Weston asked Christopher if he wanted anything. Christopher stared off, and Kate realized he faced the long center table. He couldn't see it, of course, and the direction of his gaze might have been pure coincidence. Yet Kate felt, as deep as the cold in her bones, that he sensed something over there. Maybe that's what bothered her about the gathered men. Could someone at the table be the reason they'd been drawn to this tiny village?

Weston asked again if Christopher wanted anything, even read off a few items from the menu he knew the boy liked.

No response.

The waitress came back and set out paper placemats with local business ads printed on them, then added paper napkins and silverware. Kate asked for the chicken fingers and a side of fries. Weston ordered coffee and a BLT.

"What would you like, sweetie?" the waitress asked Christopher.

Christopher began to rock. He worked his hands together as if he was trying to warm them up. Then he began to softly keen.

The waitress's eyebrows drew together. She tucked one side of her lower lip under her teeth, clearly mulling over what to make of Christopher's behavior.

Then she looked to Kate. "Autistic, huh?" She shook her head sadly and *tsked*. "More and more kids ending up like that. I think it's something in the water. The government is poisoning us 'cause they want to make us stupid."

Kate wanted to tell her it had obviously worked on her.

Weston must have seen as much. He cleared his throat. "He'll have a grilled cheese and a glass of milk."

"Sure thing." And she sailed away toward the kitchen once more.

Christopher's keening grew slightly louder.

Kate checked on him and in the process saw the man with the skinny tie headed in their direction, wearing a wide smile that showed teeth so straight and white they looked fake.

"Heads up," she said.

Weston turned in time to find the man standing at their table.

The man held his hands out in a welcoming manner. Unlike the waitress, he didn't seem the least bit fazed by Christopher's behavior. "I wanted to come over and say hello to the out-of-towners."

Kate grinned, said nothing.

Weston bowed his head less than an inch. "Hello."

"My name is Adrien LaFontaine." He said his name with a full French accent through his cemented smile. "Most folks around here have their roots in Germany or Poland. A few Irish. The LaFontaines keep them all cultured."

After a little laugh, he paused, as if expecting them to share their own bits of personal history. Neither of them said a word.

A knot in Kate's gut pulled tight. She couldn't put her finger on it, but the man unnerved her. And, while Christopher couldn't see the man, he clearly had issues with him as well. His movements became more agitated. His low whine had stopped, but he worked his hands together harder now, like he might pull his own fingers clean off.

"Would it be rude, " LaFontaine said, "if I asked what brings you to our small patch of the world?"

Kate gave her standard response. "Just passing through."

LaFontaine raised his eyebrows, which were a light brown. An earthy smell wafted off of him, as if he'd recently been digging ditches. "Passing through to where? In most cases, Coolidge is more out of the way than *on* the way."

His blunt question made Kate all the more suspicious. She would have liked to gather up Christopher and Weston and walk out of the restaurant without another word. She knew she couldn't, though. The pull would grab hold and draw them back again. For better or worse, she would have to suffer LaFontaine's creepiness until they finished whatever they were meant to do here.

Weston came to the rescue with an explanation for La-Fontaine. "I have family north of here. We're taking the scenic route."

LaFontaine's smile somehow stretched larger. A pair of dimples marked his pale cheeks. "Fantastic. You must be headed to Clinton, am I right?" His bright eyes stared at Weston while he waited for an answer.

Kate counted his uber happiness as one more reason he freaked her out.

"That's right," Weston said.

All at once, the bright eyes turned dark. His smile melted, his full lips thinning to a straight line. "Funny," he said. "There's no such town as Clinton north of here."

Kate and Weston shared a nervous glance. She couldn't figure out this man's agenda with his impromptu interrogation. She sensed he was headed toward the "We don't like strangers in our town" shtick.

Christopher went suddenly still. He turned to face Kate. She expected a psychic message from him, but didn't get one.

"Please," LaFontaine said, drawing out the word as if he were begging. "We don't need lies between us."

Most of the restaurant noise continued. The clink of silverware. The conversations. The occasional giggles from children. The men at the big table carried on without the man at the head, paying them no mind—except for the ninety-year-old man. He stared right at Kate, smiling a crooked and yellow-toothed smile. He sat there like an audience member at a play, waiting for the next plot development.

LaFontaine looked over his shoulder, then turned back, braced his hands on the edge of the table, and leaned forward. His earthy smell grew stronger, but Kate caught a whiff of his breath. It smelled like a cherry cough drop.

In only one notch up from a whisper, he said, "I know why you're here."

4

THAT'S GOOD, WESTON THOUGHT. BECAUSE I sure as hell don't.

He looked back and forth between Kate and Christopher. When LaFontaine said he knew why they were here, Kate had lost some color in her face. Weston guessed he looked a little ashen himself. But Christopher had grown suddenly calm. The boy rested his hands flat on the table in front of him. He cocked his head, as if listening to a distant sound.

"I've taken you off guard," LaFontaine said. "I apologize."

Without knowing what to say to this strange man, Weston swallowed and stayed silent.

Christopher lifted his chin, his gaze aimed toward the ceiling. LaFontaine noticed, and he went back to all smiles. He crouched beside Christopher's chair and rested a hand on the boy's shoulder.

Weston expected Christopher to pull away or at least start.

He kept still.

"The boy has the touch," LaFontaine said. "In fact, you all do, don't you?"

Weston's stomach dropped. With the number of people in the restaurant providing their body heat, the air was stuffy. Weston had started to sweat under his ugly sweater. Despite all of that, a cold chill ran up the backs of his arms and down his spine. Who the hell was this guy, and how did he know about their... gift?

Kate had that suspicious cop face on. He recognized it from the various scrapes they'd been through. It meant things were bound to get confrontational. Usually, Weston tried to defuse her. He didn't want to now. He felt a little confrontational himself. But Kate was better at it.

"What's your angle, Mr. LaFontaine?" she asked, a threat in her tone.

LaFontaine rose from his crouch and put his hands out, palms up. "No angle, Kate. I'm just the welcoming committee."

Weston's heart nearly stopped. Kate had never introduced herself.

She stood slowly. Her cheeks flushed. "How the hell do you know my name?"

"Why, Christopher told me, of course."

Weston's head spun. He had no idea what was going on here. He didn't like it. Not one bit.

He stood as well. "I think it's time to go."

Kate pointed at LaFontaine. "This guy owes us some answers."

Christopher turned to Weston, looked up at him.

A familiar itch started in the center of Weston's hand. His fingers curled, craving the feel of a pencil against them. As always, he had one in his pocket. He drew it out and sat at the table again. He felt his self-control fade. The urge to sketch took over. He flipped over the paper placemat. Its blank surface demanded him to mark it.

Pencil clutched in his fingers, Weston's hand began to skate across the paper like the planchette on a Ouija board. Seemingly random lines slowly coalesced into the beginnings of a picture, a picture matching the vivid image Christopher projected into Weston's mind.

It didn't take long for the drawing to take shape. First a roof with some missing shingles. Then an open door, what lurked beyond lost in shadow. A wraparound porch with a broken bench swing and dead vines wrapped around the railing.

When he finished, he had a picture of a large, neglected two-story house framed by a few dead maples on either side. It sat on a hill, but beyond that the sketch gave no more clues about the house's location.

Weston dropped his pencil on the table. His hand trembled slightly. His fingers had cramped. All in all, it had taken him a little over five minutes to complete the picture. An impossible task for Weston without the guidance of Christopher.

Kate was staring down at the picture. Her jaw was clenched. But the suspicion in her eyes had given way to what looked to Weston like recognition. And he had to admit, he felt as if he knew this house too, while at the same time certain he'd never seen it before.

LaFontaine laughed. "See that? I knew it."

Weston and Kate both turned their attention to the white-haired stranger.

"Knew what?" Weston asked slowly.

LaFontaine nodded at the sketch. "Why you're here. That's the Stoker place. Though the Stokers haven't lived there in forty years." He sounded nostalgic and sad. "But no matter how many folks have lived there since, we still all call it the Stoker house."

A baby cried out in that agonized way that only babies could. The child, all red-faced and teary, sat in a high chair at a nearby table. The mother plugged a bottle in the baby's mouth, cutting the crying instantly.

It was one example of the oblivious patrons who surrounded them. They had no inkling of the bizarre exchange happening at this table.

But not everyone in the restaurant was blind to them.

Weston was still looking at his sketch, but he could feel a gaze upon him. He turned in his chair.

The old man with the gap-toothed grin shamelessly stared back. His liver-spotted and bald scalp looked so thin, Weston imagined if he got close enough, he would see through to the old man's skull.

Weston glanced at Kate. She eased back into her chair, resignation in her eyes, but her face still tense with suspicion. She realized, same as Weston, that they were exactly where they were meant to be, the X marking the spot on the invisible map they'd been following for the last two days.

Then Kate snapped her gaze to Christopher. She took on that blank stare she got when Christopher spoke to her. Weston heard him as well.

He's one of us.

Weston didn't have to ask what that meant. But he did worry about the implications.

Several months ago, Christopher had guided Weston on what seemed like a fool's errand, a diversion from their mission to find the Beast. Instead, he had had a plan all along —to find Kate. Because Kate was like them, able to communicate in a different way, to experience things most people would never believe, and who had suffered losses brought on by the same mad killer.

Did Christopher plan on collecting another member to join them?

It didn't feel right. First of all, all three of them had been compelled to find this place, not just Christopher. Secondly, LaFontaine seemed far too smarmy to fit in with them.

Weston reached out to Christopher with his thoughts.

Do you know what this is all about?

Christopher pivoted in his chair toward Weston, but aimed his blind gaze out of the restaurant's front window.

You know we aren't the only ones.

Of course Weston knew this. Father Morales back in Alabama came immediately to mind. But before he could respond to Chris, LaFontaine interrupted.

"You have questions," he said. "I have some of the answers. But if I had them all, you probably wouldn't be here."

"You said you knew why we're here. Did Christopher tell you that too?"

"No," he said, shaking his head. "Folks like you always come for the same reason." He pointed at the sketch. "And I won't bother to warn you away, because you won't listen. None of you do."

"Warn us about what?" Kate asked.

He gave her a dead stare. His ability to switch from jovial to severe was frighteningly unnatural.

"That if you don't leave now," he said, "the house will kill you."

5

KATE LOOKED LAFONTAINE UP AND down. She didn't know what to make of him. She wanted to write him off as some weird liar. Her time as a cop had exposed her to all manner of bullshit artists, and she prided herself on knowing the difference. But not a single twitch or tell from La-Fontaine alerted her internal polygraph.

Besides, was his warning so farfetched?

Kate had learned from Christopher and Weston that tragedy and terror could mark a place, linger behind like a faint scent. And Christopher had a gift for catching that scent, interpreting the clues left behind.

Maybe the house held such a scent.

That did not, however, put her at ease with LaFontaine. She did not like that he felt he could communicate with Christopher without asking permission. She didn't care that he shared their abilities. Strangers weren't supposed to approach children and strike up conversations, with or without actually speaking.

She stared LaFontaine in the eye. She didn't like having to look up at him from the table, but she didn't want to draw attention from anyone in the restaurant. Kate had learned from experience that talking about weird shit in front of regular people brought the wrong kind of attention.

"Why would we care about this house?"

"I don't know. It simply tends to draw folks like you."

"Like us? You seem to be like us, but that house hasn't killed you."

He nodded. "But it tried to."

"We've seen our share of trouble," Kate said. "I think we can handle it."

LaFontaine's shoulders rose as he inhaled deeply, then released a sigh that whistled slightly, like wind through a keyhole.

"As I anticipated you would say. I don't need the touch to recognize a determined lady."

Kate didn't like the sound of that comment. She'd fought the worst kind of sexism while climbing the ranks in the Santa Flora police department. But she'd also learned to ignore it, so she let it slide.

The waitress arrived with their meals. Kate welcomed the interruption. Now LaFontaine would have to leave them alone. Finally.

But before the waitress could pass out their plates, La-Fontaine rested a hand on the girl's shoulder. "Hold on a minute, Amy." He turned to Kate. "If you'd indulge me one last request. Come sit at our table. The men you see have all lived here their whole lives. Even the young gentlemen have stories to tell."

"Thanks for the offer," Kate said, trying to sound polite for the waitress's sake. "But we can't stay long."

LaFontaine flashed those over-white teeth. "I insist."

The waitress giggled. "If Mr. LaFontaine insists, you can't resist," she sang like a car dealer's jingle.

That disturbed Kate almost as much as LaFontaine's rambling about this house. If Kate hadn't known LaFontaine had an ability similar to her and her companions, she might have missed it. But a fleeting look of concentration on La-Fontaine's face gave Kate the impression that he might be influencing the girl somehow. Not controlling her, necessarily. More like giving her an emotional bump to turn the previously harried demeanor of an overworked waitress into the giggling girl standing at his side.

You're full of it, Kate told herself. You're letting your misgivings about this weirdo get carried away.

Weston cleared his throat to get Kate's attention. He raised his eyebrows in a question.

The thought of spending any more time with this man made her skin crawl. She didn't trust him. She didn't like him. And she didn't want anything more than to eat her food in peace. As she started to say as much—using a more civilized tone—Christopher interrupted her.

We need to know.

Kate groaned internally. Things were not going to go her way, damn it.

Know what? she asked.

Christopher hadn't moved an inch in the last several minutes. Now he turned his head to face her.

What they know.

Kate looked past smiling Amy and smiling LaFontaine, over to the table of men. It wasn't just the old man staring now. Some of the others had turned in their seats or broke off their conversations to check the trio out. Their stares were neither threatening nor friendly. Just curious.

"We can pull up some extra chairs," LaFontaine said. "There's plenty of room."

"Yeah," Amy piped in. "Plenty."

We need to know, Christopher repeated.

Kate smiled and knew it looked fake. "That sounds wonderful."

6

THE MEN ON ONE SIDE of the table all shifted their chairs down to make room for the three of them. Amy cheerfully passed out their meals. And the old man, who sat across from them, grinned at Kate in a way that old men should *not* do, his gaze directed not at her face, but about six inches lower. She noticed a small but nasty-looking mole just beneath his left eye, that somehow made his stare even more disconcerting.

She had hung her parka on the back of her chair. Now she wished she'd left it on, stuffy air be damned.

From his seat at the head of the table, LaFontaine made introductions all around. There were ten other men besides LaFontaine, and no way could Kate remember all their names. There was a Bobby, an Arnold, two or three Johns—who all looked the same to Kate—and some other names that slipped right by her after LaFontaine rattled them off.

The whole time, Kate's chicken strips and fries cooled,

losing their thick, greasy aroma. The fries had probably turned soft by now. But despite LaFontaine's assurance —"Don't be bashful"—common manners kept her from eating. Meanwhile, her stomach grumbled in protest of decorum.

In his introductions, LaFontaine saved the old man for last.

He patted the old man gently on the shoulder. "This here is the oldest living resident of Coolidge Township. He's so old, in fact, that no one can remember his actual age." He grinned. "He is also lucky enough to have the honor of being my father."

The men around the table laughed, the old man included. One of the men in his forties—Kate thought it was one of the Johns—cracked, "Lucky my ass."

LaFontaine rolled his eyes, but kept his signature smile pasted on his face. "They're jealous." Then he waved his hands as if to clear the air. "Enough. I brought our friends over here because of their interest in the Stoker house."

Most of the men openly frowned. But the youngest two looked sad and a little sick.

One of the men with a gray goatee that hung three inches off his chin said, "You ain't looking to buy the place, I hope."

Kate shook her head. "Just looking."

The youngest lit up. He pointed at her. "You guys from the paper?"

Kate let a short laugh slip. Yeah, doesn't every journalist have a blind and mute eleven-year-old boy in tow?

LaFontaine gestured toward Weston. "Noah here is an artist. He likes to draw old houses."

It was as good an excuse as any.

"Well, that's kinda weird," the young one blurted.

The man next to him stabbed him with an elbow. The young man bowed his head. "Sorry."

The long table sat close to the kitchen. The sizzle of the fryer and the sound of a metal spatula scraping across the grill rang out clearly, punctuated by the cook's occasional shout, "Order up."

Christopher quietly ate his grilled cheese, empty gaze directed toward LaFontaine's father. The boy seemed separate from them. He might as well have been sitting at his own table. It didn't bother Kate any. In fact, she thought his low profile was best at the moment.

A man named Gregory—Kate remembered his name because it didn't seem to fit with all the others—cocked his head back, looking down his nose at Kate. He wore a pair of glasses with thin gold frames. His dark hair was flat on one side, probably from wearing the ball cap on the table in front of him.

"You know anything about that place?" he asked. "Because if you don't, you'll probably change your mind 'bout visiting it when you find out."

LaFontaine looked back and forth between Kate and Weston, expression full of "I told you so."

Some of the men grumbled and nodded. LaFontaine's father reached across the table and rested a liver-spotted hand on Kate's. His skin felt like cold silk. His touch was light. Despite his earlier leering, he now gave off a grandfatherly vibe that actually set Kate at ease.

"Don't let them scare you with their silly stories. The Stoker place has had its share of tragedy, but it isn't cursed. That's poppycock."

Kate smiled at his use of *poppycock*. You didn't hear that much anymore.

"Three separate murders," Gregory said.

"Four," the young man said.

"Way more than that," one of the others added, "if you count the disappearances."

Gregory nodded. "Good point. Not to mention that the four murders involved at least two folks."

The old man waved a hand. "Hush, now. What kind of gentleman tallies the dead?"

They ignored his protests. The young man counted out on his fingers. "Fifteen," he said. "I think."

"You're forgetting one of the Williams children."

"Aw, shit. You're right."

The man next to the young man elbowed him again. And the young man repeated his sheepish apology.

Kate turned to her companions to get a read on them. Weston looked like he hadn't slept in days. Which was the case, if she didn't count her shifts behind the wheel while he tried to get some sleep in the passenger seat—not an easy or comfortable task.

"Order up," the cook called out.

Christopher had left the crust of his sandwich on his plate. He had his hand on his glass of milk, but he didn't show any sign that he meant to drink it. He still stared straight ahead. His lips were pressed together. He looked lost in thought.

The men were on a roll. They started passing pieces of stories back and forth across the table. They didn't seem at all concerned about who could hear them. Some of the restaurant's patrons had started taking nervous glances at the long table.

Kate resisted the urge to tell them "All right already. We get the point." She held back not because she didn't want to be rude. She remembered what Christopher had said. And she trusted his instincts, which were more than just instincts.

So she kept her mouth shut, because they needed to know

what these men knew.

Gregory pushed his glasses up the bridge of his nose and leaned his elbows on the table.

"The killings are one thing" he said, "but what happened to the Stokers is a whole 'nother ball of ugly."

His presentation sounded practiced. Kate had a feeling these guys told a lot of stories. Instead of a campfire, they had their regular table.

He continued, "I don't know how long the Stokers go back in Coolidge. Maybe back to its founding."

"They were one of the first," another chimed in.

"Anyway, over a hundred years ago, one of the Stoker children went missing. They searched day and night for a week."

"Two weeks," John with the goatee said.

The young man shook his head. "I heard three."

"It don't matter," Gregory went on. "Point is, a child not much older than yours there," he nodded at Christopher, "went missing and weren't never found." He folded his hands as if in prayer and rested them on the table. "Few years later, another went missing. A Stoker daughter. In her teens. Folks thought she might've run off with a boy, but I doubt that."

He paused, chewing on a thought.

The waitress, Amy, rushed by, sparing them a curious glance. She didn't seem so perky anymore.

The heat had grown almost unbearable. Kate could feel sweat on her back, her shirt clinging to her skin. Hard to believe, but part of her wished she were back out in the cold.

Finally, Gregory nodded to himself as if coming to a decision. "Pretnear every five years or so after that, another Stoker went missing. And not all of them young. Oldest was forty, forty-five if I recall."

LaFontaine's father patted Kate's hand again. "Now, keep in mind, this house was in the family for a long time. Times were harder back then. The winters colder."

"Come on," Gregory said. "It ain't like they got sick and dropped dead. They plain vanished."

The old man shook his head, face scrunched up and wrinkling the wrinkles already there. "Poppycock."

Kate had to agree with him. The whole thing smelled of urban legend. Only, she supposed, this was *rural* legend. And LaFontaine's plan to scare them off had backfired. Pull or no pull, she had to check this place out or her curiosity would kill her. She didn't like not knowing the entire story. It's what had made her a good cop. Could be it was also an easy street to trouble. But she could handle trouble.

"So this whole time, the Stokers kept living there, generation after generation?"

Gregory smacked his lips. "I know. Seems crazy. But here's the crux... More than half that family disappeared with no trace. Then the last Stoker alive, probably close to the same age as Adrien's dad there, died in that house in his sleep, alone. And that was it for the Stokers."

"That sounds ridiculous," Weston said with a grumpy edge. His lack of sleep and food—he'd left his BLT untouched—were catching up to him.

The men didn't seem to notice or care.

LaFontaine's father reached across the table and patted the table when he couldn't reach Weston's hand. "That's right, son. Ridiculous, to say the least."

Kate wished Christopher had some input on this tale, but he remained silent and in the same position. She also noticed that LaFontaine had gone still. When he caught Kate looking at him, he grinned.

"Maybe so," Gregory said. "But the murders? Those are

as real as real gets."

"You said there were four killings, right?" Kate asked.

"Yep. All four were families. One married couple, no kids, they were the first to buy the Stoker house. City folk looking to take up organic farming or some bull. They renovated the house."

"Gutted is more like it," John said and scratched at his goatee.

"Anyway," Gregory said. "They lived there five, six years before it happened."

Kate sensed where this was going. "Murder suicide," she said.

"Huh-uh. Both stabbed to death. Killer never found."

"Then the Scotts," John said. "Family of four. Two little girls."

Kate felt Weston go rigid beside her at the mention of the girls. A story like this hit a little too close to home. And Gregory didn't hold back the details.

"All of 'em got it in the face with a shotgun."

John stroked his goatee, crossed his arms, and leaned back in his chair. "Killer never found."

"I'll spare you the details of the others," Gregory said. "You get the idea. Each one of them ending the same. Killer never found."

This didn't sound at all plausible. At the same time, she knew plausible had a little flex to it. The three of them lived on that flexible edge. "None of these murders were ever solved?"

"Ain't for not trying neither. Hell, the last one they even had the FBI sniffing around. Probably the most exciting thing to happen in Coolidge."

Some of the men chuckled.

"And they never found anything?"

Gregory shook his head. "But last I heard, they're still working on the last one."

Kate raised an eyebrow. "Oh?"

"Yeah. After all, it just happened... what?" He looked across the table to the John with the goatee.

"End of October," John said. "Just over two months."

7

WESTON WAS SICK OF LISTENING to a group of men describe a series of murders with thinly veiled glee. He couldn't keep from thinking about these families' living relatives, what they must be going through, trying to bury images of their dead loved ones in the darkness at the back of their minds, only to have them resurface in nightmares and daydreams. Like now, for him.

Anna. And his sweet little girls. His poor, poor girls.

He couldn't stop seeing them. Both in life and death. The images blurring together so that his happiest memories became tainted by the bloodiest ones.

It took some doing, but Weston managed to keep his eyes from watering.

"Order up."

Weston cringed. If he had to listen to that cook shout those two words for much longer, he'd make sure the next order went up his ass.

Easy there, he told himself.

He was letting his fatigue stoke his anger. The cook wasn't the problem. In fact, the problem wasn't even these men, LaFontaine, or this dinky town in the middle of nowhere. The real problem was the Beast.

Months ago, he had sent Weston a message in a very unique way, telling him how much he enjoyed this little game of "hide and seek" they had going. Yet despite the talk of murdered families, the radar ping that had brought them to this town didn't *feel* like one of the Beast's games, and Weston thought this side trip had taken them off mission.

He was about to say as much to Kate, but LaFontaine spoke first.

"It's time for me to take the old man home to bed."

"Will you tuck me in, too?" his father said with derision.

LaFontaine patted him on the back, then stood. "It was a pleasure meeting the three of you. I wish you a safe journey."

He took his father by the elbow and helped him out of his seat, although the old man moved well enough that Weston suspected he didn't really need the help. "Go get your coat, Dad. I'll be right there."

His father took a long look at his son. His eyes narrowed, deepening his crow's feet.

The two of them stared at each other for an awkward handful of seconds, then LaFontaine smiled. "Go on, Dad."

The old man nodded and shuffled over to a coat rack beside the front door.

"He thinks I coddle him too much," LaFontaine said. "Perhaps he's right. But he's my dad. What can I do?"

Out of patience, and in no mood for chitchat, Weston didn't respond. He eyeballed LaFontaine with blatant distaste. Weston didn't care if this man had "the touch," or whatever he wanted to call it. Their similarities ended there. Weston did not appreciate LaFontaine inviting them over to this table only to share gruesome horror stories about murdered families. While he had to admit hearing about the young girls had touched a nerve, it wasn't the stories themselves that disturbed Weston. It was LaFontaine's attempt to use those stories—stories of others' tragedies—to try to manipulate him and Kate to stay away from the house.

"I'm sorry if I upset you, Mr. Weston. You have to believe I only had the best of intentions." Then he bent forward and pulled something from his back pocket. He set it in front of Weston. A black leather-bound journal not much larger than a paperback. The cover looked a little worn, but when Weston opened it and flipped through its pages, they were all blank, never used.

"For your sketches," LaFontaine said. "I have little use for it anymore."

Weston wondered what use he'd had of it in the first place, seeing as he hadn't scribbled a word or drawn so much as a doodle inside. He didn't bother asking. He guessed LaFontaine's answer would only lead to more questions. Questions they didn't have time for. Weston wanted to get whatever it was that had drawn them here over with, so they could get back to what was important.

Finding the Beast.

Humoring LaFontaine, Weston took the journal and reached back to his parka hanging on his chair. He slipped the book into an inside pocket. "Thanks," he said flatly.

After a short bow, LaFontaine left them, collecting his coat—and his father—at the front door. As they slipped out the door, a shot of ice cold wind cut through the restaurant.

Weston shivered. The cold contrast against his warm face was a brisk shock.

It was only then that he became aware of the other men all staring down the table at the three of them.

The one named John, who wore a thick beard and small glasses, lifted a coffee mug in a sort of salute. "Don't mind us, now. You go ahead and eat. You look like you need it."

Kate grunted.

Weston felt the same way. The L on his BLT had wilted and looked slimy. The fat on the bacon had congealed. And his coffee had gone cold. The waitress had never come by to refill it, as if she sensed she shouldn't disturb the conversation at the table.

He checked on Christopher. The boy had finished all of his grilled cheese except for the crusts. He hadn't touched his milk, though. The whole time they sat at the long table, he had hardly moved. But now his concentrated stare broke. He lifted his milk and chugged the cheap plastic glass dry.

Weston half expected Chris to slam the empty glass down like a frat boy after shot-gunning a beer. Instead, he gently rested it back on the table.

He turned toward Weston and Kate. A small milk mustache coated his upper lip.

Adrien says the last crime scene is still at the house. Nobody's cleaned it up yet.

So Christopher was on a first name basis with LaFontaine? It confirmed a suspicion he'd had that the two had been communicating the whole time.

He leaned close to Christopher. "I don't trust a word he says," he whispered.

No, Chris agreed. *But he's scared. He's real scared.*

Kate leaned in as well. To the men at the table they probably looked like they were conspiring. Weston supposed, technically, they were.

"Of what?" he asked.

I don't know.

Then he changed the subject on a dime.

You two should eat.

Weston must have really looked like hell, with everyone telling him he needed to eat. Kate didn't look so bad, but she was younger and in better shape than him—the advantage of her being an ex-cop who still exercised whenever the three of them stopped long enough.

But Chris was right. Appetizing or not, they needed the fuel.

Kate must have come to the same conclusion. She stared down at her plate, curled her lip, and sighed. "Bon appétit."

They ate quickly and in silence.

The men at the table never said another word to them except for a quick goodbye as the three of them headed out.

Weston was glad for it. He hoped never to have to speak to any of them again.

8

THE COLD ACTUALLY FELT GOOD to Kate as they crossed the street to the Rambler, but she figured that wouldn't last long. The snowfall came down steadily, the flakes as big as quarters. Almost an inch already covered the sidewalk, and once in the car, Weston had to run the wipers to clear the windshield.

He started the car, but left it in park.

The gray sky had blackened while they'd been in the restaurant. Twilight apparently came early during a Michigan winter. The clouds hid any signs of stars.

Christopher had pulled his hood back over his head and drawn the strings so that only a small circle of his face showed. He sat in the middle of the back seat, his gaze turned downward.

"It's getting dark," Weston said. "Do we want to try to find somewhere for the night?"

That would have been the smart play. Especially if this

house was as dangerous as LaFontaine and his cronies wanted them to believe.

Kate had taken the placemat with Weston's drawing on it. She pulled it from her parka's pocket and unfolded it. That weird déjà vu struck her again. She felt as if she had seen this house in a dream once.

That tingle at the back of her skull returned. Slightly muted, but definitely there.

"I don't think I'll be able to sleep until we get a look at the place," she said. "Maybe a quick drive by?"

Weston let out a short laugh. "One problem. We never asked where to find it."

Kate gave him a flat stare. "You really think we needed to?"

A nearby streetlight cut shadows across Weston's face. His eyes looked sunken and tired. He hadn't shaved since they had started north, leaving him with a rough stubble.

"No," he said. "I guess not."

He put the Rambler in gear and pulled away from the curb. Only a few tire tracks ran down the road through the snow, and those had already begun to fade under a fresh layer.

It took barely five minutes to clear the village's downtown. They headed north, away from the single intersection, in the opposite direction from where they had arrived.

The wipers thumped back and forth.

The relief the cold had provided when Kate first left the restaurant quickly faded. She had already started to shiver. She cranked the heat, but the air hadn't had a chance to warm up yet. A blast of cool air from the floor vents curled its way up her pant legs and chilled her ankles. She drew her feet back.

"Damn it."

Weston, used to her complaints, ignored her and kept his eyes on the road. The car fishtailed slightly when he tried to accelerate to the speed limit. He eased off the gas, his leather gloves creaking as he clamped down on the wheel.

"Why would anyone live in a place like this?" Kate asked. "It's not just cold. It's dangerous."

"We're okay," Weston said. "But if the snow keeps coming down like this, we're gonna have to find someplace to wait it out. Last thing we want is to end up stuck in a ditch in the middle of nowhere."

They traveled a couple of miles before coming to an intersection. Without comment, Weston turned right. The snow had hidden it, but when they pulled onto the side road Kate could feel from the vibrations through the car that it was a dirt track.

A sparse line of maples ran along either side of the road. Night had settled in. The only light along this stretch came from the headlights. And they did little more than illuminate the swirls of snow caught in their beams.

Movement to Kate's right caught her attention. She glimpsed the white tail of a deer before it ran beyond the trees and into the darkness.

"So what do you make of LaFontaine?" she asked, hoping some conversation would take her mind off the worsening road conditions.

"He's... odd."

"Thanks for the understatement." Kate twisted in her seat to face him. "I mean, what do you think his angle is?"

"You don't think he's just worried about us?"

She snorted. "Really?"

"I don't know," Weston said with a shrug. "He went through a lot of trouble to let us know the house's violent history. Not that I appreciated his methods." He frowned. "I take back what I said. He's not odd, he's an ass."

Kate laughed. "That's more like it."

The Rambler slipped as they came down from a small hill. Weston turned into the skid and righted the vehicle before it drifted too far. The dark kept Kate from seeing his face clearly, but she sensed the tension in him. He sat forward, peering over the wheel, his elbows locked and his arms rigid.

"Maybe it's haunted," he said, voice pinched.

"You mean the house?"

He nodded. "Cursed? Haunted? Whatever it is, it's more than a string of bad luck or coincidence."

"What makes you say that?"

"Why else would we be here?"

Kate leaned back in her seat and let Weston concentrate on his driving. She tugged on her belt to make sure it held tight.

The rest of the way, they all stayed quiet. Occasionally, Christopher would sigh. Kate couldn't tell if the sighs were nervous or wistful. They sounded like a little of both.

She lost count of the number of side roads Weston turned onto. None of them were paved. Sometimes they drove between thickets of dormant trees. Other times they coasted past stretches of farmland blanketed by snow. Weston had to up the speed of the wipers to keep up with the increasing snowfall.

They passed a number of houses. A lot of them looked the same in the dark. A few of them looked big enough to match the one in the drawing. Most of them had lights on inside. None of them looked abandoned.

After a good hour they came to another hill.

The Rambler's tires spun as it tried to climb through the thick snow. Weston gave it some extra gas. The engine revved. The Rambler's back end slid sideways. Then the tires caught and they lurched forward. The dip on the other side sent them skidding. Weston pumped the brakes and came to a stop at the end of a long drive that had been obscured by a wall of pines. A gap in the pines was just wide enough to accommodate entry onto the driveway.

The headlights exposed a rusted mailbox lying on its side, so overgrown it had fused to the land.

Through the gap in the pines, Kate saw the silhouette of a large house on top of a hill about an eighth of a mile down the driveway.

"That's it," she said without hesitation.

Without a word, Weston turned into the drive. Under the snow, gravel crunched against the tires.

Unlike earlier, the heater had managed to work the chill out of Kate. But the sight of the house brought back a slice of it down her spine. Her scalp prickled. As they approached the house, an indefinable energy buzzed through her. The closest thing she could compare it to was an adrenaline rush, but without the increased heart rate or shaky thrill. And the closer they got to the house the more intense this feeling grew.

From the Rambler's backseat Kate heard a repeated thump like a loud heartbeat. She looked back and found Christopher rocking hard enough to pound his back against the seat. He clenched his hands in fists and rhythmically struck his thighs.

Weston's breathing quickened. He swiped a hand across his forehead as if wiping away a sheen of sweat.

This place was wrong. All wrong. And all three of them felt it.

"Stop the car," Kate said.

Weston didn't need convincing. He stomped the brake. The Rambler skidded a few feet in the snow then came to a halt. The idling engine sounded like the snore of a sleeping giant. A mysterious rattle from the heater started up for a handful of seconds, then stopped.

Kate could smell her own nervous sweat. An oily taste filled her mouth.

She looked toward the house, a hulking dark shape against the night sky, a slice of its vine-choked porch visible in the Rambler's headlights. Much of the porch's white paint had flaked away and let the wood underneath turn rotten from exposure to the elements.

"What are we doing here?" she asked. "This has nothing to do with the Beast."

"I've been wondering that myself."

Kate sat with her lips parted, forgotten words on her tongue. For some reason—mostly because of the strange way they'd found themselves drawn here—she had assumed this was a detour. They all had.

But what if it wasn't?

What if the Beast had set a trap of some kind?

Possible, but that didn't feel right. Kate just *wanted* this house to connect somehow, so that coming here made a little more sense than it did.

"Look what it's doing to Christopher," she said.

The boy continued his violent rocking. He had started taking panicked breaths as well.

Weston's eyes went to the rearview mirror. "Do you want to turn around? Leave?" He pulled his gaze from the mirror and directed it at Kate. "Do you think we can?"

"None of this makes sense. Not our pull to this place. Not LaFontaine. Not this damn house. This isn't how it's supposed to work."

Weston laughed, but it sounded hollow and weary. "You expect what we deal with to have rules?" He laughed again, this time strutting on the edge of hysterical. "I've learned to keep an open mind."

Kate took a deep breath and made a decision. "All right, I'll go in first. You and Christopher wait here until I give the all clear."

"Why should you go in first?"

"Because I have this," she said, patting the Beretta holstered on her hip. "And you don't."

Weston's face turned sour. He had a thing with guns, but Kate had good reasons for snagging a concealed carry permit in Texas a few months ago, and she kept the weapon on her in every state the law allowed.

The house of terror she had encountered in Houston had been a contrivance, a roadside attraction turned hunting ground for some very sick and twisted people who had gotten away with murder for years.

This place, however, was something different altogether, a crime scene with its own private horrors weighing it down. Kate was no Christopher, but she could feel them, still pulling at her.

And a gun might just come in handy.

9

KATE'S BOOTS CREAKED IN THE snow as she climbed the steps to the front porch. Along with her Beretta M9, she had also brought a Mini Maglite. She used it to check the stairs behind her. Based on the indentations she had left, at least two inches had fallen since it started three hours ago. If it kept up, or got much worse, things could get difficult, to say the least.

When she reached the covered porch, a blast of wind ran through as if she'd stepped into a wind tunnel. The cold scoured her exposed skin. Not just her face, but her hands too. In order to handle her gun, she'd left her gloves behind. But her bare knuckles had already begun to stiffen. If she stayed out too long in this, she might lose all feeling, and the gun would be useless.

On the edge of the front door, a strip of yellow police tape fluttered in the wind like a streamer. The rest of the tape must have already blown away. Instead of a knob, the door had one of those handles with a thumb latch. Kate tucked the Mag in her armpit. The handle felt like ice when she gripped it. She wondered for a moment if the door would be locked. She really didn't want to have to jimmy it open. (And maybe part of her wished it *was* locked, the perfect excuse to turn around and leave.)

No such luck.

Despite some resistance in the hinges, the door swung open easy enough.

She opened it about four inches, then retrieved the Maglite and held it level with her gun's barrel. Aiming into the darkness inside, Kate kicked the door to swing it wide. The latch rattled.

A faint but familiar smell hit her. Metallic. Rotten.

The smell of old blood and death.

Without any help from the moonlight lost behind the overcast sky, Kate had to rely completely on her flashlight. The dark house seemed to swallow the beam. It's narrow light felt inadequate and made Kate feel a little claustrophobic, as if the dark were a physical thing closing around her as she crossed the threshold.

The wind howled in through the door, nudging her like a large, impatient hand that wanted her to hurry up and get inside.

No argument from Kate. The break in the hard wind barreling through the covered porch was such a relief on her hands and face, she welcomed the shove. Once inside, she pushed the door closed behind her. The sudden silence added to the claustrophobic feel.

Quickly, she scanned her surroundings with the flashlight to reassure herself that she had, in fact, entered a large farmhouse, and not a crypt. She found herself in a small foyer. It was no wider than a regular hallway. To her right, an open door. Inside, a small den with a cherry wood desk, a dust-covered computer, and an office chair tipped on its side.

No ghosts, but the tipped chair seemed strange. A small sign of possible violence. Nothing else, though. No blood on the carpet or shattered lamps.

Directly in front of her, a stairway led up to the second floor. On the wall to her left hung a photograph, one of those over-posed portraits taken at a store in the mall. A family of three stood in front of a blue sky background with fluffy clouds, making them look as if they were floating in the sky. A middle-aged man and woman stood on either side of a boy no older than ten. All three of them had blond, almost white, hair and fair skin. Shining blue eyes. No doubt related. The boy almost looked like a mini clone of his father.

All three of them beamed, their smiles genuine despite the cheesy staged nature of the photo.

Kate felt a twinge in her gut. They looked like a sweet family. Knowing what she did about their fate gave the innocent portrait a gruesome context. She would have hated to be the one to work this scene. No matter how many times she'd witnessed brutality against families much like this one, she never got used to it. A child caught in the middle of murder rose it to a new level of awful.

Still, the tingle at the back of her skull told Kate she belonged here. Needed to be here.

No turning back.

Keeping her gun up, she crept forward and rounded the corner to the left of the stairwell.

The space opened up to a large great room. Kate had seen apartments in Santa Flora smaller than this—including her own. After the closed-in feel in the foyer, the sudden openness startled her. Granted, the flashlight didn't illuminate much more, but she could feel the expanse more so than see it.

Despite the room's size, the furnishings trended toward minimalist and modern. Not the kind of stuff she'd expect to find in a farmhouse. But she remembered LaFontaine mentioning something about a remodeling. She guessed the inside wasn't *supposed* to look like a farmhouse.

An open bookshelf made from pressboard planks on a metal frame held more statues and art pieces than books. Even the books looked more like decor with the symmetrical way they were arranged, the tallest books on either end so that they all formed a V shape. Most of the pieces surrounding the books were abstract shapes made from shiny, metallic material. A few statues Kate recognized as small recreations of famous sculptures, including the Thinker and Michelangelo's David.

She panned the flashlight to examine more of the room.

On the far side, a fireplace was inset in the wall, the mantle made from what looked like marble, and its face made of brick painted white. Ugly was the only way to describe it.

The center of the room had a couch facing the fireplace, with angular armrests and a straight back that didn't look comfortable at all. From her angle, Kate could make out one end of the glass coffee table in front of the couch. If you were going to have a set up in front of a fireplace, Kate thought you'd want something a little more cozy. But the room looked like it got as much use as the pristine books on the shelf.

Despite the layer of dust coating everything, this could have been a display in a museum.

Kate moved forward, into the room, so she could get a look at the near wall. There was a whole lot of space left on this side that she hadn't seen from the entrance. Maybe she would find something a little more lived in, though she doubted it.

Her doubts were unfounded.

Another bookshelf like the other one, only wider, was perched in the exact center of the wall. Besides some art deco styled bookends, this shelf actually held nothing but books. They also weren't arranged as neatly. And the entire bottom shelf looked like it held strictly children's books. Many of the books were paperbacks with cracked spines and the names of bestselling authors emblazoned on them. Beside the shelf sat a plastic bin full of Legos.

So real people actually had lived here. Only they hid that evidence around the corner, as if they wanted to trick visitors into thinking they were exquisitely tasteful before breaking the illusion once fully inside.

Weird. But what family didn't have its own quirks?

Kate's sure as shit was no exception—mostly because of her father.

Kate continued her assessment of the room, tracing the beam across the bookshelf to the far corner, then stopped abruptly, sucking in a sharp breath.

She nearly shrieked as the flashlight revealed a man's familiar face, though she almost didn't recognize him with the ear muffs and stocking cap hiding his white hair.

"Hello, Kate," LaFontaine said as casual as if she'd come in for a cup of coffee and a chat by the fire.

10

THE RATTLING FROM THE RAMBLER'S heater had turned into a buzz and came more frequently as Weston kept it running. He turned on the dome light and eyeballed the gas gauge. The needle sat too close to E for his tastes. If he kept the engine running for too much longer, he wasn't sure they'd have enough gas to make it to the nearest station.

While driving to the house, he had let his mind wander. It was kind of like driving to work, where you knew the way so well you didn't have to pay as much attention.

Only Weston hadn't known—not consciously—the way to the house at all. So he wasn't exactly certain how far they had strayed from the village. In fact, he wasn't sure he could find his way back.

Christopher had fallen still in the back seat. He had his eyes closed, but sat ramrod straight, so Weston didn't think he was asleep. This wasn't typical. When the boy drifted off into the haze, he usually moved, at least a little. But nothing about this trip to Michigan was typical.

Wind buffeted the Rambler hard enough to gently rock it. Each gust sounded like the wake of a passing freight train. Runnels of melted snow ran down the windshield, but the storm had picked up enough that the warmth from inside the car couldn't keep the other windows clear. Even with the dome light on, Weston felt as if he were sitting in a cave. He also felt as if the cave could collapse and bury them both.

Irrational, he knew. Probably a symptom of his growing claustrophobia. Not normally an issue for him. The piling snow, however, felt more oppressive than mere walls.

He hunkered down in his parka and folded his arms with his gloved hands tucked in his armpits. Either the heater was weakening, or he'd caught Kate's weakness to the cold.

He felt bad keeping Christopher cooped up as well. The boy's parka and gloves hadn't left the shopping bag in back of the wagon since they had picked them up in Toledo. He refused to wear them. And though he didn't act like it, he had to be freezing in just his hoodie. Even in top shape, the Rambler's heater couldn't kill all the cold.

Weston checked the dash clock. Kate had left the car twelve minutes after seven. It was now seven twenty-two. Only ten minutes. And he knew she could take care of herself. Probably better than Weston could. But he had hoped for some kind of signal from her. The last sign of her was the glow of her flashlight on the porch. Through the heavy snowfall, he couldn't make out much more than that. A hazy silhouette at best.

Then the light had disappeared from view. She had entered the house.

He thought of going after her, but he couldn't very well leave Christopher behind in the car. If he wanted to go in, he would have to take Christopher into the storm with him.

Not going to happen.

He decided he would wait another twenty minutes max, then he would drive off to get help. He tried not to think about the fact that the closest neighbor was probably three miles away or more.

Twenty minutes, Kate.

Please get your ass out here before that.

11

KATE'S WHOLE BODY TENSED. INSTINCT kept her gun trained forward, aimed at LaFontaine's chest. Her breath puffed like smoke in the cold air. But a dose of adrenaline kept her warm enough.

"What the hell are you doing here?"

He flashed his white smile, which was so out of place he looked near insane for it. He held his gloved hands out, palms up. "One final plea."

Kate wrinkled her brow. Was this guy serious? "You came all the way out here to sit in a dark, freezing old house for who knows how long, just to try and warn me away?"

He tugged at the lapel of his wool coat. "I'm used to the cold. I was raised in it. Besides, I'm wearing thermal underwear."

Thanks for the over share, Kate thought.

"This is bullshit. What are you after? Are you just crazy?"

He wore a long knit scarf wrapped around his neck all the

way up to his chin. It made him look like he was stuck in a hunched shrug. "Possibly," he said. "But that's beside the point."

Then something occurred to Kate, which made this encounter about ten times more bizarre. "I didn't see a car outside. How the hell did you get here?"

"I live next door."

An interesting fact Kate tucked away in case she needed it. It didn't answer her question, though. "There is at least twenty acres surrounding this place. You mean to tell me you walked here?"

"Of course not." He waved a hand toward the back of the house. "I rode my snowmobile. I parked it in the pole barn."

Kate blinked, shook her head as if she could rattle together some logic to all of this.

No go.

Unless...

"I'm starting to wonder," she said, "if you aren't somehow responsible for all the death in this place. Are you a serial killer, Mr. LaFontaine?"

He burst into laughter. Hollow laughter, like a man playing along with a joke he didn't understand. He templed his fingers and rested the tips against his chin. "Why would I want you to leave if I were a killer?"

"Because you're afraid we'll find something."

"But why wouldn't I just kill you?"

Kate lifted her gun a little. "Because I could kill you first."

This whole time, his smile had not faltered. It did now. But only enough to hide his teeth. "Have you done a lot of killing, Kate?"

"I'm not afraid to if I have to."

"How many have you killed?"

Was she really having this conversation? In an abandoned

house? In the middle of a goddamn blizzard?

"What has that got to do with anything?" She shook her head. "Never mind. You answer my questions. I'm not interested in yours."

"That's hardly fair."

Kate inched forward. She noticed the light quivering across his face. Her hands were shaking. The bastard had her rattled, and that pissed her off. "I'm gonna ask you one more time," she said. "What is your game?"

Even as she moved toward him, the light in his face didn't seem to bother him. He didn't so much as squint.

"I like chess," he said. "And poker, believe it or not."

"I don't want jokes," she barked. The edge in her voice sounded a little out of control. After all the weird things she'd seen in her travels, she would have thought a kook in a house wouldn't bother her. But this was about more than a white-haired weirdo. She knew that much.

LaFontaine made a surrendering gesture. "I apologize. I suppose I'm looking for levity where there isn't any."

"Funny, I thought you were trying to deflect my questions with sarcasm."

"I've answered your question several times already." He eased up to his feet, gaze on the gun in her hand.

Kate shuffled back, though he wasn't within reach. As harmless as he might look, extra caution couldn't hurt. Many a psychopath was the quiet, friendly neighbor who had never hurt a soul.

"I'm not going to hurt you, Kate. I'm trying to save your life."

"A bit dramatic, don't you think?"

"You haven't seen the mess in the kitchen."

While she was out of the wind, the general cold had continued to numb her fingers. She kept her trigger finger along the side of the gun—you didn't put it on the trigger unless you meant to pull it—and felt like it might fuse to the metal like a wet tongue to a cold flagpole. The stiffness would hamper her reaction time.

Why she thought she had to worry about this, she wasn't sure. LaFontaine didn't look like he was hiding a machete behind his back. In fact, he kept his hands held slightly away from his body and visible. The proper pose to keep from getting shot.

"I can't stay here much longer," LaFontaine said. His voice held a little quiver.

Was he afraid?

Of what? Her gun?

For some reason, she didn't think so. Something else had him spooked.

Ghosts in the house?

His shoulders sagged. He hung his head and sighed. "I'm sorry I couldn't change your mind."

"If you think you're riding off on your snowmobile without giving me some straight answers—"

A wave of dizziness spun her head. She staggered backward. The flashlight's aim drifted sideways, leaving LaFontaine in the dark. The floor felt like it was tipping. The sensation lasted all of ten seconds before she recovered.

Had LaFontaine done something to her? She couldn't see how. He hadn't twitched.

"What's going on?" She swung the light back.

The beam cut through the dark and landed on the empty recliner.

She swung the beam around, searching the room.

But LaFontaine was gone.

She was about to call out to him, then something hard struck the back of her head.

The flash of pain through her skull was the last thing she felt before blacking out.

12

THE AIR FROM THE DASH vents barely felt lukewarm. Weston's legs had grown stiff and cold. His hat and parka kept his body warm enough, but that wouldn't last long if the heater finally conked out. The clicking coming from behind the heater's control panel had become a steady buzz. Weston expected it to crank to a grating halt and quit completely any second now.

He dug his cell out of his pocket without much hope. Sure enough, no bars. Weston had started to share Kate's disdain for this winter wasteland. These days, no cell service was a deal breaker when it came to choosing a place to live.

Assuming he ever got the chance to settle down again.

He couldn't imagine it. Pursuing the Beast had become so much a part of his life, he felt as if he'd been doing it forever. What would he do when (if) that time came? Rent an apartment? Move into a new house? Live alone as a recluse? Or would Christopher stay with him? Would Kate?

No. He couldn't picture it. And there was no point. He'd burn that bridge when he came to it.

Weston twisted in his seat to look at Christopher.

The boy had loosened up somewhat. No longer sitting so stiffly. A short, gentle rocking. Weston's eyes had adjusted to the dark enough to see the boy's eyes were open, but the shadows distorted his expression, making him look wicked —not how Weston would ever describe Christopher normally.

He turned back to check the clock. Eight-fifteen. Five minutes past the twenty-minutes he had given Kate.

He sighed. He couldn't wait any longer. Not only would the Rambler run out of gas, but he couldn't justify keeping Christopher out in this cold another minute.

He reached for the gearshift, and—

Catcatcatcatcat.

The force of Christopher's voice in Weston's head shot through like a migraine. He winced.

"Chris, easy. What's wrong?"

Catcatcatcat...

It sounded like he was saying *cat*, but that didn't make any sense. Sometimes the boy's messages came through distorted, like a... well... a bad cell phone signal. Obviously, it wasn't the lack of a nearby cell tower warping his message. Christopher's panic must have been working against him.

Weston replied to Christopher with his mind. *Calm down. I can't understand what you're saying.*

The boy moaned. He was scared. Not only did Weston hear it in the sound of his moaning, he *felt* it deep in his chest, as if Christopher were sharing his fear through a similar channel as his thoughts.

Catcatcatcat. Cat. Cat. Caaaate.

Then Weston heard it right, the signal suddenly clear.

Kate.

She had to be in trouble. But before he could process this, the sound of the rear passenger door snapping open was followed by a blast of cold wind carrying a flurry of snow. The dome light came on.

Weston spun in time to see Christopher launch out of the car into the storm.

"Christopher," he shouted.

But the boy had vanished into the darkness and snowfall.

He'd left the door open behind him. The wind roared in and scattered snow across the back seat.

What the hell was he thinking?

Weston threw open his door and charged out into the storm. The frigid wind hit him hard and took his breath away.

Between the night and the heavy snowfall, Weston could barely see a thing. He couldn't even see the house. How the hell could he find Christopher in this mess? And what about Kate? He felt powerless and angry at the storm. Angry at himself for letting Kate go into that fucking house alone. And absolutely livid that he had let Christopher get away from him so easily.

But he couldn't even feel the burn from that anger in the oppressive cold.

Fists clenched, his gut tense and churning, he ran blindly into the swirling white chaos.

"Christopher?" The wind swallowed his shout. He tried again with his thoughts.

Christopher? Where are you?

No response.

He looked behind him. He had left the Rambler open, the engine running (but so what? A tank of gas wouldn't do a thing to help them now). The wagon's inside light barely cut through snowy haze. The snowflakes had turned small and hard, pelting his face, cutting against his cheeks.

He turned in a circle, searching for any kind of landmark.

Nothing.

Maybe he could triangulate the location of the house based on the position of the Rambler. But when he tried to find it, the vehicle's light was gone. Either the battery had died or the electrical had gone on the fritz. The old girl had failed him, leaving him disoriented, his sense of direction broken. Cut off from Christopher. Useless to Kate.

He shouted into the dark storm.

They were seriously fucked.

13

LIGHT.

EVEN WITH her eyes closed, it hurt.

And confused her.

She thought it had been dark.

She opened her eyes. She had to squint against the flood of light coming from above her. Her head throbbed. The back of her skull felt wet. Her arms were pulled behind her, the itchy feel of rope around her wrists, binding them together. A hard pole pressed against her back. She sat on a hard, cold surface. Before her eyes adjusted to the light, she already had a picture of her predicament. Thoughts of Houston came to mind.

When her vision cleared, she saw pretty much what she expected. Concrete walls, marked in places with rust and water stains around cracks. The floor was also concrete, painted a flat gray. Bare wooden joists above her. A long fluorescent light hung from one of the joists from a narrow metal chain.

A basement.

The air smelled of paint and turpentine.

Something shuffled to her right. Kate turned and found LaFontaine sitting on a metal folding chair fifteen feet away. He had Kate's gun in his hand, only he held it flat on his palm like a dinner plate. He had removed his ear muffs and cap. His white curls were mashed down, giving his head a sort of mushroom look.

Unlike usual, he was not smiling.

Anger simmered in his eyes. His frown drew lines in his face like parentheses around his mouth. "I hope you're happy."

Behind him sat a workbench, nicked and scratched, the wood dark in spots and rubbed shiny in others. It looked like an heirloom, well used by several earlier generations. To the right of the workbench was an open door to the staircase. More light poured in through it.

Light.

It didn't make sense.

Was she still in the farmhouse?

LaFontaine must have recognized her confusion. "I have a genny," he said. "We turn it on whenever we use the house between residents."

Kate's throat closed. She had to swallow a couple times before she could speak. "Who's *we*?"

He grunted. "Probably shouldn't have said that."

Her initial disorientation cleared as anger cut through her. "What the fuck is going on?"

"You already know," he said. "More or less."

Her increased heart rate made the pain in her head pump in time with her pulse. She caught sight of an old-fashioned Louisville Slugger leaning against the workbench. The bat had a red smudge on its wide end. Blood.

Her blood.

"You son of a bitch. You're the killer."

He stared at her silently for a long time, his eyes shining in the harsh light. Then he sucked his teeth. The wet smacking sound grated and made Kate's skin crawl.

"There aren't any more answers for you, Kate. I gave you all I could." He stood. Pocketed her gun. "Now it's time to fatten you up."

Kate's stomach dropped.

Fatten her up?

None of the men at the table in the restaurant had said anything about cannibalism. But Gregory had also spared them any details of the more recent killings. Still, how much could he fatten her up? He couldn't really plan on keeping her in the basement long enough to force feed her, or whatever he had planned.

Could he?

He started for the staircase.

"Wait," Kate shouted. "What's going on? LaFontaine, what the hell are you doing?"

He didn't respond. When he reached the door he looked over his shoulder. He looked sad. Resigned. Then he sighed and hit a switch just inside the stairwell.

The basement lights went out.

"LaFontaine!"

The only light left came from the doorway to the stairs. He crossed through and closed the door behind him.

Now only a swatch of light came under the space at the door's bottom.

The sound of his footsteps, heavy from his boots, thumped up the stairs.

Kate heard him stop, guessing he'd reached the top.

Then the light coming from under the door winked out, leaving Kate in an impenetrable darkness.

She shouted out to him once more, but the last sign of him came from the creaking of the floorboards above as he walked away through the house.

Silence.

Except for the sound of her blood rushing in time to her pulse. A sour taste filled her mouth. Her breathing got away from her. She jerked her hands against the pole she was tied to, thought she felt some give, but the rope still held.

She pulled harder.

The effort awakened the pain at the back of her head. Her eyes watered.

Fuck.

But the rope slipped a little more.

Or was that her imagination? Wishful thinking?

The rope rubbed her wrists raw. Between the friction and her sweat, it felt like she'd developed a painful rash.

Still, she pulled harder.

A little more slip.

Pain crackled through her hands. She wished they were still numb from the cold, but LaFontaine had apparently turned on the heat along with the lights.

She didn't care if she had to rip the skin off her hands to get loose. And once she did, she was going to use that Louisville Slugger to knock out that fucker's perfect teeth and then cave in his skull.

Leaning forward for more leverage, Kate yanked the rope between her wrists against the pole. She clamped her mouth shut, cutting off her panicked breaths and used that energy to pull with all her might. The pain was nearly unbearable. If the ropes didn't give soon, she would have to ease off and give herself a chance to rest before trying again.

Tears streamed down her face.

Her wrists felt ready to break loose before the ropes.

A little more slip.

"You're going to hurt yourself."

Kate shrieked at the sound of the voice coming out of the dark. Startled, she quit pulling. Her efforts to get free had raised her heartbeat. It kicked up twice as fast now.

It was a woman's voice, but Kate hadn't heard enough to know much more.

"Who's there?" she called.

A soft hushing came from Kate's left, the sound like a mother comforting a fussy child.

The sound didn't comfort her a bit. It raised the hairs on the back of Kate's neck and sent a shiver up her spine.

"It's me, Kit Kat," the woman said.

And before she said more, Kate recognized the voice, as impossible as it was.

"It's your mother."

14

WESTON STOOD IN THE MIDST of the ripping wind and endless white. No sign of the house. No sign of Christopher.

He felt so cold his bones seemed to shiver. The snow on the ground was halfway up to his knees by now, making every step a precarious and slow stunt where he could trip and face plant at any moment. The wind in his ears stung and deafened him to everything but its freight train *whoosh*.

He must have gotten twisted around. He could only guess how far he might have wandered from the Rambler or the house. He could stomp around in the storm forever without finding any shelter. His heart pounded as he imagined someone discovering him after the storm, frozen solid in the middle of a field, wearing a permanent mask of pain.

That was good. Think happy thoughts.

Imagining his death wasn't the worst of it, though. His pointless death in the middle of a blizzard meant failing Anna. It meant the Beast slipping away without falling to

Weston's vengeance. It meant his whole life after losing Anna was a complete waste.

It also meant failing to protect Christopher.

He wouldn't stand for that. He had to fight, to keep slogging until he found his way to the boy or collapsed in the effort.

He arbitrarily turned to his right and started dragging his feet through the snow. The muscles in his calves and thighs burned. His damp jeans, however, chilled his skin. Snow had snuck its way down into his boots as well and soaked into his wool socks. Sweat and melted snow squished between his toes.

Stop.

The voice spoke in his mind the same way Christopher could. But it wasn't Christopher's voice. It belonged to a woman, and the sound brought him to a halt. A cold tingle ran over his head and down his neck.

Noah, come this way.

Though the voice was in his head, it also somehow came from behind him. He didn't want to turn around. He was afraid of what he'd find.

It was *her* voice.

Anna.

This way, Noah. You have to come this way.

He squeezed his eyes shut and turned. The wind tugged at him, made him dizzy. The cutting snow scoured his cheeks.

Come to me, Noah. You'll be safe here.

Slowly, he opened his eyes. He made out a shadow through the relentless snowfall, but that was all. It moved away from him, starting to fade into the white.

Weston charged forward, huffing, his body weak and shaky. His heart rate had grown so heavy his heart felt swollen and ready to burst.

That's right, Noah. This way.

The moisture in his eyes froze as it reached his cheeks. His face was an icy mask. His joints were stiff. But he kept pushing forward, following the shadow.

And Anna's voice continued to coax him forward.

Then the shadow melded into a larger silhouette. Much larger.

Weston's foot struck something hard in the snow and he dropped to his knees. Jags of pain shot through his kneecaps. He cried out. But he didn't wait for the pain to pass. He swept the snow away from what he'd tripped on and revealed a wooden step.

He let loose a throaty cheer.

Anna had led him to the house.

15

SHE'S NOT REAL, KATE THOUGHT.

A trick of her mind. A symptom of panic. Nothing more.

She had experienced something like this a few months ago in Texas, a street bum speaking to her in her mother's voice. An unnerving moment she had attributed to stress and the sudden changes in her life.

And this was the same thing.

Wasn't it?

She felt something brush her cheek and started at the touch.

"I've missed you, Kate."

Kate clenched her jaw. She wouldn't engage with this hallucination. Wouldn't allow it to tempt her to believe the impossible.

She redoubled her efforts to pull out of her bindings.

Her mother *tsked*. "You won't even talk to your own mother?"

"You're not real," Kate barked in spite of her promise to herself. The distraction had interrupted her attempt to free herself. She refocused and tried again.

"I'm real enough," her mother said. "I'm right next to you."

Kate's face swelled as she pulled with all her might, holding her breath, ignoring the voice in the dark. She growled through the cuffs of pain around her wrists. Now she wasn't sure if there was any more give. She wasn't sure she could trust any of her senses, considering she was hearing voices.

Well, not *voices*. One very specific voice.

Kate relaxed, gasping. The rope burn had spread up her arm. The raw pain felt worse when she stopped tugging, allowing it to steal back her attention. LaFontaine had tied her up with her parka still on. It felt like a broiler inside. Sweat slicked every inch of her torso. The odor wafting off her body smelled like the inside of a gym locker.

"You have to listen to me," her non-existent mother said. "You owe me that much."

Kate grunted. This hallucination was getting tedious. But no matter how unreal it was, Kate found it hard to tune out her own mother's voice. It had been so long since she'd last heard it.

No, she thought. I can't let it get to me.

She went back to pulling. A little more and she could get out of this basement, away from the lying darkness.

"It's your fault," her mother said. "You let me die."

Kate stopped struggling.

"I was just a girl," She felt stupid for talking to something that wasn't there, but she couldn't help herself. "What could I have possibly done?"

"You should have protected me. You should have protected your little brother. He never even had the chance to be born."

"No." Kate felt a pinch in her chest. What this voice was saying proved it did not belong to her mother. Her mother would never say such a thing. But it still hurt, because it did *sound* like her. "Leave me alone."

"And you should have taken better care of your father. He suffered so much when he was sick, but you treated him like a burden, not a man."

Kate clenched her teeth. She couldn't let this thing get to her. She had to focus on getting out of there.

"I think," her mother said in a philosophical tone, "death follows you, Kate. You inspire suffering."

"My mother would never talk to me like this."

So why was she bothering to argue with a lie?

"Now you have a new family. A cute little trio of misfits. Freaks."

"Stop it."

"And they will die too, Kate. You take that poor little cripple to places of death. You expose him to danger. You *pursue* danger." Her mother hummed thoughtfully. "Do you *want* him to die?"

"Shut up." Kate clamped her mouth shut, threw her body forward, and wrenched against her bonds as hard as she could. Her anger exploded inside her, gave her an extra jolt of power that overwhelmed the pain.

One hand ripped free. Momentum caused her to pitch forward and she hit the floor on her side, crunching her arm underneath her. Her elbow knocked against the concrete, adding a jag of pain to her already screaming wrists.

"Well, look at you," her mother said. "Not that it will do much good. The little boy is going to die here, Kate. And your male friend too. You are all going to die here."

With an angry growl, Kate pushed herself up on her feet.

The rope still hung from one wrist, but with her other hand free it had loosened enough for her to pull it off. She threw the rope aside and heard it knock something over with a clang. Something metallic. She was pretty sure the sound came from the workbench. If she could feel her way through the dark to the bench, she could easily find the light switch by the door.

Fill the basement with light; obliterate the voice in the darkness.

"I love you," her mother said from behind her. "You're going to die, but I love you."

This hallucination had a serious case of split personality.

Kate ignored the voice and staggered through the dark until she bumped against the workbench. The smell of turpentine was so strong it made her eyes water and her nose burn. That's what she must have knocked over with the rope.

As she expected, it took nothing to follow the wall to the light switch.

She turned. When the lights came on, she wanted to see the empty basement, she wanted to witness the hallucination disappear along with the dark.

She flicked the switch.

The sudden light stung her eyes and made her squint.

So she didn't trust what she thought she saw standing by the pole she had been tied to.

But her eyes adjusted.

And the figure remained.

Her mother.

Standing in the middle of the basement.

She looked as beautiful as Kate remembered. She wore a pinstriped dress with thin purple lines. Her hair was pulled back in a braid. Her face looked as soft and her eyes as sweet as ever. She was a memory made real.

Kate's breath caught. Her legs went weak and she had to lean against the wall to stay standing.

"Oh, Kit Kat," her mother said. "You're in for a rough night."

16

WESTON COULDN'T BELIEVE HOW WARM the house felt.

At first, he thought maybe it was just the stark contrast between standing in the brutal wind and coming out of it. But it was too warm for that. In fact, it was *comfortable*. He didn't care about *his* comfort, though. He hoped like hell Christopher had found his way here. The danger the boy had sensed may have guided him to Kate.

May have did not satisfy Weston one bit. He'd be damned if he'd let anything happen to Chris. And he'd be damned if he'd let this pointless deviation from their search for the Beast derail their whole quest.

He stood at the back of the great room, by the bookshelf opposite the fancy fireplace and the fancy couch in front of it. He heard a sigh from a nearby vent in the floor and started at the sound.

What on earth was the heat doing on in an abandoned house?

Had LaFontaine fooled with them? Was the family in the portrait in the foyer still living here? Was this some wicked joke? If so, LaFontaine's sick sense of humor had put Christopher in danger. If (*when*) they got out of this, Weston was going to rip out a hunk of that son of a bitch's puffy, white hair.

While the great room was dark, a light was on deeper in the house that illuminated things enough for Weston to see his surroundings. The light came from around a corner through an archway that probably led to a dining room. From his vantage point, he could see the end of a dining table covered in gray dust.

While most the furniture in the great room had a stark symmetry to it, a well-worn recliner in the corner had an indentation in the seat as if someone had recently sat there.

A hard knot tightened in Weston's gut at the possibility that someone was still living here, and Weston had invaded their home.

Of course, that didn't jive with the pull they had felt that brought them to this house in the first place. It also didn't explain why Kate hadn't come out to get them so they could get out of the freezing car and into warm shelter.

Occupied or not, there was still something unusual about this place. Maybe even something dangerous.

"Kate?"

His voice echoed in the silence.

He waited a second, hoping he'd get a response, but not really expecting one.

Nothing.

He crossed the great room, trailing snow off his boots on the way. After spending so much time in the dark, the dining room light stunned him a little as he entered. The light came from an austere chandelier—if you could call it that—comprised of a saucer-shaped shade and a narrow, two-foot long cylinder keeping it mounted to the ceiling, all of it made from brushed steel.

The style choice of the light didn't match the table at all. The table was made of polished cherry wood with four matching chairs. Ornately carved spindles made up the seat backs, and the seat cushions were plaid. This collection of furniture had the farmhouse look Weston had expected to find inside. He wondered if it was a hand-me-down the family couldn't bring themselves to get rid of.

Kind of like his Rambler.

A square, ceramic vase sat in the table's center. A bouquet of wilted lilies hung limp over the edges of the vase.

Straight curtains covered the window on the other side of the table. The hard snow skittered across the glass like dozens of tiny insects. A creepy sound in an otherwise plain old dining room.

If Christopher was still out there, he would freeze to death. Weston could only hope that the boy had also managed to make it into the house—he'd certainly been headed in this direction—but then, where was he?

In any case, he had to prepare for the worst. If he planned on going back into the storm, he needed to find a flashlight, maybe a blanket or quilt to wrap around the boy.

The dining room opened directly into the kitchen, an L-shaped island demarcating where one began and the other ended. He thought he might find a flashlight in one of the drawers in there.

He made a cursory assessment of the kitchen—gray cabinets, stainless steel appliances, a dry rack by the sink with a couple plates and a glass still in it.

Something on the island caught his attention.

At first he thought it was a spill. The stain had a brownish tint like cocoa. But when he stepped aside and let the dining room light reach past him, he saw the stain was more a rust color. It was also less like a puddle. More of a streak across the tile surface that ended at the far edge.

Considering the circumstances, Weston had little doubt he was looking at dried blood.

Part of him wanted to round the island and see what lay on the other side. Another part thought of that portrait in the foyer, and the little blond boy.

He hesitated.

Not that he would find any bodies back there. Those would have been removed, autopsied, possibly still stored in the morgue. One thought led to another, though. The story of the little girls supposedly killed in this house years before. And that brought Weston back to his own girls.

He shook the thoughts loose. He'd dealt with crime scenes where children had been murdered. This wasn't any different. Besides, he had one *living* child to worry about right now. He pushed past his hesitation and rounded the island into the kitchen proper.

And gasped.

Almost the entire floor was covered with the same colored substance as on the island. The streaks on the island continued over the edge on this side and ran down the face of the built-in cabinets. From there the stain spread, stretching to the far corner and flush along the baseboards under more cabinets. The floor looked painted with it. Only the edge of the tiled section at Weston's feet escaped coverage. That was the only way he knew the floor was linoleum.

Additional spatters dotted the cabinets, and another streak drew a shallow U across the kitchen counter.

He was surprised that someone hadn't gone through and cleaned up after the murders. Maybe the family hadn't had anyone close by to take care of things. So after the police left the house behind, the mess remained untouched.

How incredibly sad.

As much as he hated to do it, if Weston wanted to go through the drawers looking for a flashlight, he would have to walk on the blood. When he stepped forward, the moisture on the soles of his boots wetted the blood like watercolor paint. He grimaced and tried not to look down. He only made it halfway into the kitchen when he heard a voice.

Anna's voice.

"He's safe, Noah."

He spun toward the sound, but didn't see anyone there.

He'd heard her, though. And not in his head this time. It had sounded like she was just on the other side of the island.

Tentatively, Weston said, "Anna?"

"Come here," she said. Now it sounded like she was in the great room. "I'll show you. Christopher is safe."

Normally, Weston wouldn't trust the voice of a dead person. Especially after the ones they'd encountered in Alabama and Florida.

But Anna had guided him to safety when he was lost in the storm. She was communicating with him—though he didn't necessarily believe it was really Anna—and had proven herself helpful. Maybe she had led Christopher to the house as well.

Weston came out of the kitchen and hurried into the great room.

Empty.

"Here," she said from the foyer.

The heat had worked out all the cold in him. Now he was sweating. He unzipped his parka and tucked his gloves in his pockets, his hand touching the journal LaFontaine had given him.

"I'm coming," he said. He felt a little foolish, but part of him hoped somehow that this really was Anna. That he was talking to her... ghost, or spirit.

But such things were usually Chris's territory, not his. Did this house have some way of allowing communication with the dead?

"Noah," Anna said. She sounded farther away. Muffled. "Hurry."

He charged forward. Right now, he would focus on the moment, and leave the questions for another time.

He reached the foyer and yet again faced disappointment. No sign of her.

"Up here," she called from the shadows at the top of the stairs.

He strained to see through the darkness, but the dining room light only went so far.

"Anna?"

"Christopher is up here. He's desperate to see you." After a small pause, she said, "I am, too."

Weston moved to climb the stairs when a scream from somewhere deeper in the house made him freeze. It sounded like Kate.

"Noah," Anna urged. "You have to hurry."

He backed away from the stairs. He looked out into the great room, then back upstairs. He felt himself pulled in two directions.

"That's my friend," he said. "I have to help her."

"*No*." The voice sounded wet and angry. It drew up a bad taste in Weston's mouth. That wasn't his Anna. They'd had their fair share of rows over the course of their marriage, but anger had never twisted her voice like that.

It was enough to break his tenuous trust.

He clenched his fists and hurried back the way he'd come.

His heart felt as if it were sinking into his gut.

"If you leave, I won't let you see the girls," Anna shouted after him, her voice buzzing in the narrow stairwell.

He swallowed the rock in his throat and kept going.

Even though he knew she was a lie, next to saying good-bye to his family forever, walking away was the hardest thing he'd ever had to do.

17

NO, NO, NONONO.

Too much.

Looking across the basement at her mother, Kate felt the scream bubble up her throat. She couldn't hold it back. And when she let it loose, her throat burned from the strain.

Her mother opened her mouth, about to say something more.

Kate wouldn't hear it. Refused.

She spun and scrambled up the stairs. She could barely breathe. Her heart raced.

She couldn't tell if it was fear that shook her, or anger. Probably some of both. Once she started up, she didn't look back. Another door blocked the top of the stairs. When she reached it, she cranked the knob and slammed her shoulder against it, flinging the door open as she burst through it.

She swung the door shut and leaned her back against it, panting.

Get a hold of yourself, Kate. She's a trick. Part of whatever game LaFontaine is playing.

The explanation sounded right, but it didn't comfort her much. If LaFontaine could mess with her head, make her actually *see* her dead mother, what else could he do? Mind control?

But if he could control her, he wouldn't have had to tie her to that pole.

Her chest ached from her heavy breathing and pumping heart. She focused on calming herself, all the while expecting her mother to try the door. Calming herself also included getting her head back to rational thinking. If her mother were simply a projection from Kate's mind, she damned well couldn't open doors.

She found herself in a laundry/mud room. A shiny red washer and dryer sat side-by-side under a row of hanging cabinets. On the floor underneath the door to the dryer, a basket held neatly folded towels and some plain white T-shirts. A relic of normal life before the family's murder.

Another door led outside. Wind beat against it as if desperate to come in.

To her right a narrow archway led to a breakfast nook with the kitchen probably around the corner. The light helping her see came from somewhere beyond there.

The nook had a small table with only two chairs. A teddy bear with a split in a seam by the ear, showing some of the stuffing inside, sat on the table, propped up by a toy tank. Beside these were a stack of school books and a loose-leaf binder. It looked as if the nook doubled as a study area for the blond boy in the photograph, the teddy bear a comforting relic from his younger days.

Kate smiled. The innocent display helped her come down —as long as she could keep away thoughts about how the boy would never sit at that table again.

Loud footsteps thumped toward her in a full run, breaking the moment.

LaFontaine?

She instinctively went for her Beretta and came up empty. LaFontaine had it, and if that was him barreling toward her, he might just use it.

She glanced around for some kind of weapon. Even a broom would be better than nothing. But it looked like nothing would have to do, unless she could defend herself with a laundry basket.

The footsteps came to an abrupt halt.

"Kate?"

A wave of relief ran through her. It was Weston.

She came out of the laundry room and found him standing in the space between the kitchen and dining room. The light came from a hanging lamp above the dining room table.

Weston's face lit up when he saw her. He hurried toward her, and for a second Kate thought he might pull her into a bear hug. She thought she might not mind either. But he came up short, breathing heavily.

"Are you okay?" he asked. "I heard you scream."

As much as she knew she had every right to scream at what she had seen downstairs, her face flushed knowing Weston had heard her. She glanced past him and her stomach dropped.

"Where's Christopher?"

"I don't know. I—"

"You don't know?" Her muscles tensed so hard they felt like they might snap. She clenched a hand into a fist. It took all of her will not to throw that fist into Weston's gut. "How can you not know? You just left him behind?"

"Would you listen?"

"Shut up. We have to find—"

Something banged behind her and a wicked rush of cold air blew out of the laundry room with enough force to ruffle her hair.

She whirled around, an irrational thought flitting through her mind—*it's my mother*—and saw Christopher barrel in through the open back door.

He hugged himself as he stumbled forward, violently shaking. A crust of snow covered him from head to toe. The small section of his face uncovered by his hood was so red he looked sunburned. When he reached the middle of the laundry room, he dropped to his knees.

The sharp smell of ice blew in from outside. Even with her parka still on, the touch of the wind drove the cold through Kate's entire body. She rushed to Christopher and dropped to his side, then wrapped her arms around him to give him as much warmth as her body could provide.

Weston had come to the entrance to the laundry room, but stood there with a stunned expression, unmoving.

"Get the door," Kate shouted.

He snapped out of his daze and ran to the door. It took some visible effort to push it against the wind and get it latched. His parka had been unzipped, but once he had the door closed he wrenched the zipper up. A single hard shiver shook him.

Christopher felt like ice against Kate's chest. He trembled in her arms. His blue lips quivered and he moaned softly, his voice undulating in time to his shivering.

Weston knelt on the other side of him and wrapped his arms around the boy and Kate both, sandwiching Chris between them.

Kate's anger flashed anew. "How could you leave him out in that? Why wasn't he with you?"

"We were in the Rambler," Weston said. "He started blasting your name over and over. Then he bolted out of the car." He swallowed, guilt plain on his face. "I tried to go after him but the storm... I got lost."

The thought of Christopher out in the cold, alone, simultaneously burned Kate around the neck and chilled her low in her belly. She wanted to blame Weston, chew him out. But she knew Chris had a mind of his own, and an uncanny ability to take care of himself despite his limitations. The boy could sometimes take his self-sufficiency for granted.

Still, she couldn't let Weston off the hook completely. "You got lost, but you managed to find your way to the house just fine."

That typical weariness returned to Weston's eyes. With both of them hugging Christopher, their faces were only a handful of inches apart. Kate stared directly into his eyes and saw more than weariness. She saw fear.

"I didn't find my own way," he said. "I was led."

Christopher cried out. He started rocking so hard Kate had to tighten her hold on him to keep him from pitching forward onto the floor.

She bent her head to try to see his face, but couldn't see past his hood. "What is it, Chris?"

Lucy. She's back.

Kate glanced at Weston. His face had turned to stone.

She's here somewhere. Somehow she got away from the Beast.

Kate's stomach twisted.

Weston shook his head. "It's a trick, Christopher. It wasn't really her."

I heard her. She helped me find the house.

Weston closed his eyes and sighed.

"It happened to you, too," Kate said to Weston. Not a

question. Just looking at him, she knew she was right. "It was Anna, wasn't it?"

His face pinched. He nodded.

"I saw my mother," she said. "In the basement. I *saw* her."

"How is the house doing this?"

"It's not the house," Kate said. "It's LaFontaine."

He cocked an eyebrow. "What makes you say that?"

"Because he's here. And he's a hell of a lot more dangerous than he looks."

18

THEY GRAVITATED TOWARD THE LIGHT, gathering at the dining room table as if sitting down for a board meeting. Christopher sat at the head of the table with Weston and Kate on either side.

Kate had pulled a couple towels from the laundry basket and wrapped them over Christopher's shoulders like blankets. Melted snow had already soaked them through. He continued to quiver. Not as violently, thank heavens.

The sight of the dead flowers in the vase made Kate shove the vase to the far side of the table.

Their meeting convened, they caught each other up on what they'd been through since their arrival. Their stories had an eerie similarity, especially Christopher's and Weston's, both guided to the house by their lost loved ones. The pattern was stark enough. Each of them had been haunted by those they had lost to the Beast. LaFontaine had managed to find their deepest wounds and cut them fresh.

Weston stopped Kate almost immediately after she started recounting her experiences.

"He was just sitting there? Waiting?"

Kate nodded. Then went on a bit more before Weston stopped her again.

"You had a gun on him. And he still managed to slip around you?"

The impatient sigh, she hoped, sent the message that she didn't want to dwell on that point. She felt foolish enough as it was.

Message received, Weston held up his hands. "Sorry. Go on."

She did, and got through the entire story without another interruption. The whole time, Christopher sat quietly, gaze forward, hands folded in his lap, irregular shivers making him jerk as if poked with an electric prod.

He'd shared his own tale first, with few words.

I sensed Kate was in trouble. I didn't think about the storm. Or Noah. I just acted.

I got twisted around.

Then I heard Lucy. She took my hand. Led me to the house.

At this point, he paused. His Adam's apple bobbed.

Then she was gone.

And that was the end. He hadn't shared any more.

It nearly drove Kate to tears. He sounded so certain it really *was* Lucy.

But in reality, she was traveling with the Beast. At least they hoped she was. For all they knew, he'd dumped her broken body on the side of the road somewhere.

He had taken her the same night he had attacked the group home where Chris and Lucy had lived. Killed everyone. Thought he'd killed the boy. Then took Lucy, a little girl with Down syndrome, like a trophy, or a pet. It was too disturbing to imagine.

Until a few months ago, Chris had been in psychic communication with the girl. But shortly after Kate had joined him and Weston on the road, that communication had been abruptly cut off and they still didn't know why.

After Kate finished talking, the three of them sat in silence, chewing over their situation. So many questions. Not the least of which was why the hell was LaFontaine doing this?

Weston broke the silence first. "Just what are we dealing with here?"

Kate released a long breath through her nose. "A psychopath with psychic powers."

"Not just one. He said *we* when he was talking to you. So there's at least one other person involved. Maybe more."

Kate remembered the group of psychos she'd encountered in Houston and shivered at the thought. What the hell was happening to this world?

"The guys in the diner?" she asked. "The ones at LaFontaine's table?"

"All of them?"

"Who knows?"

"But they were all trying to scare us away from the house. LaFontaine included."

"You're right. It doesn't add up. No argument from me."

Weston dragged his hands down his face and groaned. "So what do we do? Go room to room, looking for him?"

The question irked Kate. "Haven't you listened to a word I said? I had a gun on him, and he got the better of me. Now I don't even have the gun."

"Then we're screwed? We wait here until he comes to get us?"

"We definitely stick together. We'll have an easier time of keeping each other focused when he starts filling our heads with more b.s."

"But then what?"

Kate shook her head. How could they fight something that attacked them from within their own minds? Especially with more than one person behind the scheme? Especially when they didn't even understand what the scheme was?

"We need more information," she said. "We're working from a place of ignorance."

"What kind of information? From where?"

I can gather, Chris said.

Kate and Weston both turned to him, and Kate's tongue carried a bitter taste.

"I don't think that's wise," Weston said.

Why not?

"Because," Kate told him, "we don't know the nature of LaFontaine's abilities."

"Gathering might make you vulnerable to him," Weston said. "Besides, according to the stories, this house has seen a lot more death than any you've gathered from before. We're talking generations. It could overwhelm you."

It might not.

Kate leaned toward Christopher. He couldn't see her, but she knew he could sense her closeness and, hopefully, her concern. "I can't take that risk."

Christopher wrinkled his nose.

It's not your risk to take.

Weston put a hand on the boy's shoulder.

Christopher shrugged it off.

Neither of you is my boss. I can make my own decisions.

Then he stood. He pulled the towels tightly around his shoulders.

Are you gonna help me or not?
Kate looked to Weston.
He shrugged.
"All right," she said. "Where should we do this?"
Weston didn't hesitate. "The kitchen."

19

WESTON GUIDED CHRISTOPHER TO THE edge of the kitchen. The blood was still muddied at the spots where Weston had stepped earlier. He also noticed his red boot prints on the carpet that circled the island and led back into the great room, each step a little more faded than the last.

The iron stink of all that blood turned his stomach. He caught a taste of his BLT from the restaurant. Swallowed back the urge to gag.

Kate stood just behind him. "So that's what he meant."

Weston looked back at her over his shoulder. "How's that?"

"LaFontaine. He mentioned a mess in the kitchen."

"Mess." Weston grunted. "That's one word for it."

Christopher shed his towels. His gray hoodie was dark with melted snow. He smelled damp and sweaty.

I'm ready.

Then he walked into the kitchen and stopped dead center.

The light from the dining room lost some of its strength at this distance. Shadows crept across the boy's face as he turned in a slow circle.

He stopped turning when he faced the kitchen sink. He tilted his head back and drew his hood off. His hair was matted down against his skull.

Weston knew the exact moment when Christopher entered gathering mode. He could read small tells he had picked up after watching the boy do this over and over during their search for the Beast. His hands going stiff at his sides. A certain tilt to his head. His gaze on the ceiling. A distinct cadence to his breathing.

And the rocking. Always the rocking.

Now it was just a matter of waiting to see which one of them Christopher would choose to receive and interpret what he gathered.

He backed up to stand at Kate's side.

After a minute or so, Weston felt the tug. He absently reached into his pants pocket and withdrew his pencil. Then he reached into his parka pocket and pulled out the blank journal LaFontaine had given him.

As if touching the journal's leather cover was a switch, images flooded Weston's mind. Too many to focus on and interpret, let alone draw. Normally he would slip into his own trance at this moment, but that didn't seem to be happening.

Christopher's breath shuddered.

"What's going on?" Kate asked.

Weston couldn't answer. He was too busy trying to process the tidal wave of imagery pouring across his mind's eye. He drifted over to the island where he set the journal down not far from the wide streak of blood, and flipped it open to a random page. He poised his pencil above the paper. He suddenly needed to draw. The sensation was as urgent as a full bladder.

But the images wouldn't stop coming.

He couldn't draw.

All at once, the imagery stopped. His mind had turned as blank as the page in front of him.

"What the hell?"

He looked up.

Christopher no longer stood in the kitchen.

Weston turned.

Kate no longer stood at the kitchen's edge.

Neither of them were anywhere in sight.

There was something else different. It took a second for Weston to register the increased lighting.

The kitchen light, a large white dome on the ceiling, was on.

The metallic scent of the blood hung thicker in the air. When Weston looked, he noticed the streak on the island was bright and wet. He heard a steady patter as the blood dripped off the counter and onto the kitchen floor.

He peered around the island, gut twisting at what he might find, afraid it would be the young boy, but his relief at finding the boy's father instead was diminished by the sight of the gore on the floor.

A hot coal burned in Weston's throat, the taste of bile rolling up from the back.

The father's bright blond hair was almost entirely dyed red with blood. He lay on his back. His eyes were rolled in the back of his head, mouth agape as if he couldn't believe he'd just been murdered. At first, Weston thought the man's legs were twisted at an impossible angle, the knees pointed sideways.

His eyes had tricked him, not ready to process the whole

truth about this slaughtered man.

But he quickly realized the man wasn't twisted. He was severed in half at the waist, mangled entrails spilling out the bottom of his belly to fill the gap between his two halves.

Weston slapped a hand over his mouth as he retched. He tried to breathe slowly through his nose, but was assaulted by the stink of feces and blood, which made him retch again.

He turned away and sucked air through his mouth as he pinched his nose shut.

His stomach churned. He almost vomited. Barely kept his food down.

After a few seconds, he had his gag reflex under control.

This had to be another one of LaFontaine's tricks. Weston didn't have visions when Christopher gathered. He drew pictures. That was his role. This...

This wasn't right.

He let his hand fall away from his nose. The smell still pushed its way up his nostrils. He took careful, shallow breaths, trying to grow desensitized to the stink. After he thought he could keep his BLT down, he turned to face the kitchen once more.

His heart stopped for a second.

Two others now occupied the kitchen. A snuffling woman, her blouse soaked in red, her cheeks smeared with it, her tears drawing lines through it. And the man facing her, his back to Weston.

Dangling from the man's hand at his side, a chainsaw grumbled as it idled. The smell of gasoline mixed with the death scent. A wicked combination that had Weston's gut writhing all over again.

Though the man's back was to Weston, Weston had no trouble recognizing the white curls on his head.

LaFontaine.

He wore a white button-down shirt with the sleeves rolled up. Blood matted down the hair on his forearms. The cuffs of his charcoal slacks looked like he'd waded through a pool of it.

Blood, blood, and more blood.

Weston had never seen so much at once.

LaFontaine raised the chainsaw and revved it. The chain spun and the engine's whine reverberated against the walls.

The woman screamed and tried to back away, her arm drawing a streak of blood in a wide arc along the counter top. But LaFontaine closed in on her and penned her in the corner.

He let the chainsaw go idle again. "Do you still see your sister?"

The woman looked over his shoulder, her eyes focused on something that wasn't there.

Weston had a good idea what was going on. Like La-Fontaine had made Anna appear to Weston, Kate's mom to her, and Lucy to Christopher, he must have had this woman seeing her sister. Probably a dead sister. Or at least lost to her in some way.

Was that LaFontaine's ultimate strategy? Haunt a person with a lost loved one before murdering them?

"Do you see her?" LaFontaine asked again.

The woman nodded, her gaze still directed beyond him to an empty space four feet to Weston's side.

"Good," LaFontaine said. "You should be nice and fat."

Then he raised the chainsaw and started the chain spinning and the motor keening. He closed in.

The woman screamed and shook. Her eyes went from LaFontaine to the empty space and back to him. She cried out some words, but the chainsaw drowned her voice. Weston couldn't understand what she'd said.

When LaFontaine was within reach, he lifted the chainsaw and brought the blade down onto her skull.

Weston closed his eyes and shouted.

Something touched his shoulder.

He jerked. His heart kicked.

It wasn't until he spun around and saw Kate standing there that he realized the house had fallen silent.

Kate's hand hung in the air. She was the one who had touched him.

Panting, Weston forced himself to check the kitchen, part of him convinced the vision of that woman's murder would return, and he would catch sight of the chainsaw cutting through the top of her head.

But only Christopher stood there, shadows across his face, his blank gaze directed at Weston with a clear look of concern.

Kate rested her hand on Weston's back.

"Noah, what happened?"

He hung his head. Every time he blinked, he could see the husband cut in two on the kitchen floor, the obscene amount of blood, the wife's petrified stare at someone who wasn't there, while LaFontaine brought down the chainsaw.

"I... I was there."

"Where?"

His face was hot and sweaty.

Something snapped between his fingers.

He looked down in time to see his broken pencil fall to the floor.

His legs didn't want to hold him anymore. He leaned against the island, saw the journal sitting there. The leather binding had pulled the book shut. He nodded at it.

"LaFontaine didn't give that to me to draw in," he said. "Chris's gathering triggered it somehow. Made me see La-

Fontaine's butchery as if I was there."

"Do you mean the kind of thing *I* usually have?"

"Yeah. For whatever reason, the journal had me seeing things instead of drawing them."

Kate pressed her lips together and shook her head. Then she put her hand on the journal and slid it closer.

"Not instead."

PART TWO

"Good men but see death, the wicked taste it."

~Ben Jonson

20

THE WHOLE SIGHT HAD TURNED Kate's skin to gooseflesh.

Weston's arm jerking madly as he drew something in the journal, his back to Kate, the drawing out of her view. The sheen of sweat on the back of his neck. The quick glances toward the kitchen as if whatever he was sketching was in there.

Maybe it was.

But worse than these sights was the noise he made. A quivering and wet whimper that sounded childlike. She knew before he came out of his trance that this time was different for him. Though she never would have guessed he'd entered a vision of the murder. That was her territory.

Weston looked down at the journal as if it might strike like a cobra if he reached for it. The experience had clearly shaken him. And she couldn't blame him. There was a massive difference between seeing the artifacts of a murder left behind after its completion, and actually standing in the room, watching a person kill another.

She waited a moment, then asked him to tell her what he saw in his vision.

He pulled his gaze away from the journal to look her in the eyes. His sunken and haunted expression looked ten times as intense as usual.

"He used a chainsaw."

Only four words. But enough to raise the hairs on the back of Kate's neck. He didn't have to say more for her to fill in plenty of her own imagined details.

"Okay," she said carefully. "Forget the description. Did you learn anything?"

He explained LaFontaine's apparent MO. Taunt his victims with visions of lost loved ones, then at the peak of their distress, brutally murder them. Then he mentioned something that sparked Kate's memory.

"He said she was fat?" Kate asked.

Weston nodded. "But not her weight. It had something to do with her seeing her sister that made her 'fat.'"

"When I was tied to that pole, he mentioned fattening me up."

At some point, Christopher had come over to stand at Weston's side. Kate had been so focused on her conversation, she hadn't noticed the boy come out of the kitchen. A track of red footprints from his sneakers ran alongside the set Weston had left behind earlier. The boy faced toward the back of the house.

Kate had a sense that he was remembering what had happened to him while he'd been outside.

Weston said, "I think it's pretty obvious what he means now."

Kate chewed on her lip, nodded. "He gets off on turning a

person into an emotional wreck before killing them. Not exactly original behavior for a serial killer."

"Only his method of terrorizing victims has a psychic twist."

"Which is why he draws in people like us. We're more receptive. He can root around in our heads and make us see things in ways normal people can't."

Weston scrunched up his face and frowned. "You think he's what pulled us here? From over a thousand miles away? That's quite a reach. A scary fucking reach."

"Maybe it really is the house. The house draws them in like a web, then LaFontaine comes in, wraps them up, and eats them."

Christopher nodded. *That sounds right.*

An idea—an ugly one—sprang to Kate's mind. "You think it's more than just getting off? You think he gets something more from... feeding on these people?"

Kate meant it as an open question to either of them, but Weston turned to Christopher as if waiting for his opinion first. The boy, after all, was their resident expert on all things psychic.

I think it's possible. Maybe.

Kate wasn't sure how this distinction could help them, but it was good to know an enemy's motives.

We still need to know what Noah drew.

He was right. And Weston seemed to have come out of the worst of his shakes.

"You want the honors?" she asked him.

Weston picked up the book without a word. He riffled through the pages and stopped toward the middle. His brow creased. He tilted his head to one side while studying the page.

He had the journal up with the spine facing Kate, so she

couldn't see what he was looking at, what had him so perplexed. And her curiosity chewed on her nerves.

"What is it?" she asked.

"*Who* is it," Weston said and turned the journal around so she could see.

The sketch featured a woman in a cotton dress, standing in the middle of a field. Her belly was swollen as if pregnant. She smiled, staring at something in the distance beyond the edge of the page.

She was clearly happy. For some reason that disturbed Kate more than if Weston had drawn another death scene.

"Another of LaFontaine's victims?" she asked.

Weston drew in a long breath, then slowly exhaled. "She wasn't in the vision. The woman I saw was the one who lived here last."

"So maybe it's one of the previous residents. That dress looks a little old-fashioned."

"But why would I draw her?"

A sudden burst of frustration went through Kate. She snatched the journal off the island, snapped it shut, and waved it at Weston. "Why did LaFontaine give this damn thing to you in the first place?"

"Another way to fatten us up, I guess."

"That doesn't fit. He's using people we *know* to mess with us. Not strangers. Why give you something that would clue you into what he's doing?"

"I think you're trying to force logic into a hole it won't fit."

Kate blinked.

All she did was blink.

But suddenly Weston was gone.

Christopher was gone.

Nothing else about her surroundings had changed. The

blood in the kitchen was still dry. The shadows covered the same places. Silence filled the house. And she still held the journal.

"Weston? Christopher?"

It didn't take a genius to know this was another of La-Fontaine's ruses. Somehow, not only did he have the ability to make them see things that weren't there, he could make them blind to things that *were*.

Jesus Christ, what had they gotten themselves into?

She shoved the journal in her pocket.

"Weston."

Kate turned in a circle, froze when she came to face the breakfast nook.

Her mother sat at one of the chairs at the small table. She held the stuffed bear in her lap, idly picking cotton batting from the split in the bear's seam.

"Your friends are dead," her mother said with a musical lilt as she pulled loose more of the bear's stuffing.

"Bullshit."

Out came another bit of cotton pinched between her mother's fingers. "If you want to get technical, they're still alive right *now*. But the next time you see them—assuming you do —they won't be breathing." She smiled and looked up from her slow murder of the child's toy. "They probably won't even be in one piece. I like it when they come apart."

With one quick wrench, Kate's mother twisted the bear's head and ripped it from its shoulders. The wicked smirk on her face was a sacrilege to the memory of Kate's real mother.

Kate clenched her fists, took a deep breath. Getting her worked up was exactly what LaFontaine wanted. She'd be damned if she would give him the pleasure. "You're not going to fatten me," she said. "It won't work."

Her mother tossed aside the bear's head and body. Stood.

She smoothed the skirt of her dress. "I'll admit, your little crew has more grit than I'm used to. You seem to have a better sense of your gifts than the oblivious idiots who usually come to the house."

"Probably should let us go then," Kate said. "You don't want to get hurt."

Her mother laughed. The humor never touched her eyes. "I'm not worried about getting hurt. Just the opposite. Your strength only makes the reward of breaking you down that much sweeter. You'll be twice as fat when I finally feast."

Kate's instincts had been right. This game was about more than terrifying a victim before the kill. LaFontaine fed on them somehow. To what end, she couldn't guess. Not that it mattered. The son of a bitch wouldn't be making a meal out of her.

"Who're your partners, LaFontaine? Are the men from the restaurant helping you do this? What's in it for them?"

Her mother sauntered out of the nook. Her face looked right. Her figure was right. But her posture, her gait, her body language was nothing like Kate's real mother. Apparently, LaFontaine couldn't get *everything* right.

"Is this an interrogation, Kate?" She held out her hands. "You want to cuff me? Your own mother?"

"Stop the games, LaFontaine."

Her mother shook her head, feigning sympathy. "Oh, honey. This isn't a game. This is survival of the fittest."

Then she leapt at Kate, her hands curled into claws. The claws found Kate's neck.

Kate tried to knock her away—

How could she knock away a hallucination?

—but her mother's fingers dug in. She squeezed. Impossibly, she began to choke Kate.

As impossibly, Kate grabbed at her mother's wrists. She

could feel them. As if real.

Kate could also smell her mother's breath, like dead roses.

Her mother drove her backward until Kate's spine struck the island, eyes wide and crazed as she continued to crush Kate's throat. She leaned forward until her lips touched the cup of Kate's ear.

"Keep underestimating me," she whispered. "It'll make this easier."

Kate drew in one leg, then pistoned it outward, shoving her boot into her mother's gut.

Her mother grunted and fell back onto her ass. Her hair had pulled loose from its braid. Locks stuck to her sweaty face.

Kate should have kicked her again, knocked her out. But even though it wasn't really her mother, she couldn't bring herself to do it. Besides, just because she could—or imagined she could—touch the illusion, she doubted she could knock it unconscious.

Instead, she spun and ran. She sprinted through the great room, toward the foyer, and into the den.

She slammed the door shut.

Locked it.

And waited.

She strained to listen, but didn't hear anything.

She stared at the door knob to see if it would turn. Realized how dumb that was. If this was all in her head, and her head was locked in the den with her, then the damn vision of her mother could join her without opening the door.

But she didn't reappear.

Kate counted out three minutes before letting herself relax a tiny bit.

LaFontaine had proved his point. He could make these visions seem so real, they could do physical damage. Kate's raw throat was testament to that. Could have been a psycho-somatic kind of thing. Her brain convincing her body that what she felt was real. But the actual mechanics didn't matter. What mattered was that she was at LaFontaine's mercy.

Keep underestimating me.

She couldn't. Not anymore.

21

ONE MINUTE, HE WAS TALKING TO Kate, Christopher at his side.

The next... he was alone.

That fucking LaFontaine. His tricks got more elaborate at every turn. But Weston knew they were exactly that. Tricks. Which meant Kate and Christopher were still with him, whether he could see them or not.

"Kate?" He lurched forward to where she had been standing, expecting to collide with her.

Hoping to.

He stumbled ahead and kept going. Either he had passed through her as if she were a ghost, or she had moved.

He held his arms out and slowly turned like a kid in a pool with his eyes closed playing Marco Polo. He waded through the empty air back toward the island, to where he last saw Christopher. He waved his hands out blindly. His hands passed through the air without touching a thing.

Damn it. How could LaFontaine be doing this?

Did he warp Weston's vision? Making him think he was heading in one direction while actually moving in another?

"You think too much," a voice said from the direction of the dining room.

A familiar voice that sent chills rippling down Weston's spine. He had no doubt who he would see when he looked toward the sound.

Anna sat in one of the chairs at the table, facing Weston. One hand idly brushed the table top back and forth as she smiled.

"You always did overanalyze everything. Sometimes I thought you were better at sawing logs than living life. Like you left your head in that saw mill, except for Sunday mornings at church."

Weston shook his head. "Anna never thought such things."

"How can you be sure?"

"Because I know my wife, and—"

"*Knew.*" Anna stood and came around to lean back against the end of the table. "Past tense, Noah. I'm not alive anymore. You let that monster slaughter me and the girls."

The breath Weston sucked in was hot and tasted like... like sawdust.

He set his jaw. He wouldn't let LaFontaine goad him. If the prick wanted to cut him up with a chainsaw, he'd have to do it while Weston looked him in the eye with a cold, dead stare. Not as the simpering wreck LaFontaine thought he could turn Weston into.

"Is there a point to this?"

Anna pushed away from the dining room table and came toward him. Everything about her movement, from the sway of her hips to the soft glide of her gait, matched Anna's identically. He knew she was a lie. But he couldn't get his heart to admit it. It was hard to fight the twinge around his eyes urging him to let go and cry. His face muscles ached as he tensed against the urge.

"The point," Anna said when she reached Weston, "is this."

She raised a hand and stroked Weston's cheek.

The feel of her skin against his stubbled face broke something loose inside of him.

Her touch.

He could feel her touch.

It was too much to resist.

He closed in and wrapped his arms around her, pulled her body against his, pressed his face into her hair, smelling that jasmine shampoo she had always used. Yes, this Anna was a lie. But she was a convincing lie. One he could hold and smell and feel the heat of her body and the delicate touch of her fingers against his scalp as she toyed with the hair on the back of his head.

Her breath against his neck.

The heartbeat in her chest.

A lie.

But one he was desperate to believe if only for a moment.

"God, I've missed you so much."

"I missed you, too." She hugged him tightly. "The girls, too. They have missed their daddy so very, very much."

A lie.

A damned lie.

He didn't care. He could enjoy this. Why shouldn't he? If LaFontaine wanted to give Weston as realistic a reunion with his family as he could ever wish for, why not turn it against him? Why not enjoy it instead of fear it? The asshole probably never thought of that. That Weston could play along, play the same game, and not let Anna haunt him, but comfort him instead.

"Can I see the girls?"

Anna pulled back so she could look up at Weston. Her brows pulled together and her mouth was on the verge of a pout. She used to look at him that way after an argument, when the dust had settled and he offered an apology. It meant she wasn't quite ready to forgive. But she would. She always did, his lovely Anna.

Such a small detail. It was nearly impossible to think she wasn't real.

"I don't know, Noah. You abandoned me when I was calling to you. Abandoned me for another woman."

"You know it wasn't like that. She's a friend. I was worried about her."

A corner of Anna's mouth turned up. "A friend? Noah, you could never lie to me, but you did manage to lie to yourself pretty good at times."

"It isn't like that." He pulled her closer. "I don't want to talk about Kate. It's you I want to be with right now."

"But you don't believe in me."

There it was. LaFontaine testing Weston's doubt. He didn't like Weston playing along. That wasn't how this was supposed to work.

Weston smiled, cupped her cheek with a hand. "I believe enough."

Her smile blossomed so perfectly, so much like Anna's. Her eyes shined. "I'm so glad, Noah." She put her hand over his. "We can be a family again, if only for a little while."

"That's all I want."

She took his hand in hers and moved away, gently tugging him along. "Then let's go see the girls."

22

THE WIND MADE THE HOUSE groan. Kate stared out the den's window, which faced the front of the house. She could make out the porch railing and one of the beams supporting the roof, but beyond that, swirling, impenetrable white. The moon must have been full up above the storm. The faintest glow gave the whitewashed night a ghostly cast.

Kate still had her parka on. LaFontaine still had the heat on. But looking out the window, listening to the wind tug at the house's siding, smelling the cold off the glass pane, turned her California blood to cold mercury in her veins.

She drew the curtains shut and turned away.

Once the fear of her mother's reappearance passed, Kate had turned on a floor lamp in the corner of the room. She could have hit the switch by the door to bring on the overhead light from the ceiling fan, but felt for some reason that that would be too much. As if it might draw attention. Not that LaFontaine didn't already know exactly where she was.

The floor lamp left some shadows untouched, but it provided plenty of light to see by.

At Kate's feet lay the tipped office chair. Just beyond that, the desk with a sleek but dust-covered Mac. The flat screen had streaks across it, smeared by a small hand.

The decor was neutral. Family photos hung on the wall opposite the desk so that whoever sat there could look past the computer screen and see them. A shelf with some sports memorabilia—a Detroit Tigers pennant from their World Series win in '84 (an antique now), a baseball on a short pedestal with autographs on it, a hockey puck emblazoned with the Red Wings symbol on it.

Then there was the framed needlepoint hung on another wall. It featured a small house with a heart above it. The words, HOME IS WHERE YOU HANG YOUR HEART, were stitched above the heart.

So the den was probably used by the whole family.

She lifted the office chair back onto its casters. Four divots in the carpet marked where the chair normally sat. Kate returned it to its regular place, then sat down. The faux leather creaked under her weight. The right armrest had a tear in it, but judging from the browned padding revealed by the split, the tear had been there for a while.

A ridiculous thought crossed Kate's mind. With the electricity working, she could turn on the computer. Maybe the house still had Internet. Surely the service would have been canceled after the murders—if for no other reason than the bills weren't being paid. Yet something inside her—that sixth sense she had learned to trust—told her to at least try. Mistakes could be made, and she had a very strong feeling about this.

She switched on the computer and watched it quickly boot up and come to life. But she didn't have to open a web browser to test the Internet service. An indicator showed that there was no network connection.

Shit.

The whole idea had been a foolish waste of time anyway. Even if she could get a message out, no one could make it to the house. No cars could get here, and anyone riding something like a Sno-Cat would be hard pressed to avoid crashing into a tree or dumping into a ditch.

No, they were on their own with this one.

The computer hummed. Kate stared blankly at the glowing screen. She thought about what Weston and Christopher were going through. Especially Christopher. LaFontaine had made the boy as lost to her as if she were stumbling out in the blizzard. And she could only imagine how LaFontaine was taunting him with illusions of Lucy.

She could leave and try to find them. Surely LaFontaine couldn't keep her blind to them indefinitely. Could he really be that powerful?

She guessed not. Otherwise her mother would be in the den with her, spouting more bullshit. He could only keep his show going for so long. And even if he had help, putting on a show for all three of them at once had to be draining.

Had to be.

Should she wait him out a little longer then?

Tough call. Truth was, she had no idea what LaFontaine was capable of. But she couldn't sit around and wait for the other proverbial shoe to drop either.

Pulling herself out of her hypnotic stare at the computer, Kate actually *looked* at the screen. "What the..."

A file folder stared back at her with the label, FOR KATE.

Another damn trick. The file probably wasn't even really on the computer. She was just imagining it.

She pushed away from the desk. The chair's casters

caught in their impressions in the carpet, making the chair tilt back before rolling loose.

"I'm not gonna play," Kate said to the empty room. "I'm done being the lab rat running through your maze, you hear me?"

But the folder pulled her gaze like gravity. FOR KATE. Her eyes kept snapping back to the screen after only a few seconds of looking away.

The bastard must have had a good look in her head. He knew the buttons to push, what made Kate itch. An itch that would be damn hard for her not to scratch.

No wonder curious cats had nine lives.

Unfortunately, Kate only had one. And if she didn't act, she might lose it.

But act how?

Take the bait and see what it might reveal?

Or walk away and find her own clues?

Wandering the house without aim opened her up to attack. Better to stay put if she had something right in front of her to look at.

"Fuck it."

She scooted the chair in, grabbed the mouse, and clicked on the folder.

Within the folder was a single file. A black and white image. At the moment it was a tiny thumbnail, but Kate thought it might be a wedding photo.

Of the couple who had died here?

She opened the file.

After a hesitant grunt from the computer, the picture came up on the screen full-sized.

Sure enough, it was a wedding photo, but nothing taken recently. Not even close. The thing had that faded, vintage quality, a stamp on the bottom right corner proclaiming it had been taken by LUTZ PHOTOGRAPHY, 1902, and the bride and groom's hair and clothing and stiff smiles certainly reflected the era. A title in fancy script said they were MR. AND MRS. JACQUES LAFONTAINE.

Kate did a double take on the groom.

Wait now. This didn't make any sense.

The man in the photograph was clearly a much younger version of the old man she'd seen in the restaurant today— Adrien LaFontaine's father. The features were unmistakable, especially that small, nasty-looking mole beneath his left eye.

Yet the guy had to be at least thirty years old in this photograph. Maybe older.

In *1902*?

That would make old man LaFontaine over a hundred and forty years old.

The man she'd seen in the restaurant sure as hell wasn't a teenager—but a hundred and forty? How was that even possible?

And how did this fit into anything she had been through since coming to the house?

For whatever reason, LaFontaine wanted Kate to notice his father. A father who could not be alive. Not naturally, at least. Yet she'd seen him with her own eyes, leering at her from across that restaurant table.

We turn it on whenever we use the house between residents, LaFontaine had said, raising the question of what he meant by *we*?

And what was it her mother had said?

You'll be twice as fat when I finally feast.

Until now, Kate had assumed the feast was meant for LaFontaine. She had thought it was LaFontaine speaking to her through her mother.

But maybe this wasn't about the *son*.

Maybe Adrien LaFontaine was merely the lackey. The errand boy.

What if it was his *father* who needed to draw energy from people with psychic sensibilities? Maybe "feeding" on them somehow slowed the aging process and kept him alive, like sipping from a psychic fountain of youth. Which would explain why the stories of the Stoker house reached back so far, well beyond Adrien LaFontaine's lifetime. His father had fed on the Stokers. And when he ran out of Stokers, and the house drew in more people receptive to his mental manipulations, he began feeding on them.

Was she extrapolating too much?

When she looked again at the groom's face, at those unmistakable features, it seemed that this the only explanation that made any sense.

The doorknob rattled.

Startled, Kate glanced up at the door. She shot to her feet.

The metallic jiggle of a key in the lock.

Then the door swung open and LaFontaine entered, her gun in hand.

23

ANNA LED WESTON UPSTAIRS. THE upper floor had a hallway that stretched the length of the house, illuminated by a tulip-shaped glass lamp hanging from the ceiling. Three bedrooms and a bathroom fed off of the hall. All the doors were open except for the one at the hall's far end. It was stark red with a chipped white frame.

Weston wondered fleetingly if LaFontaine was holed up in that room.

The wallpaper in the hall was a cheery yellow patterned with daisies. Nothing you'd expect to find based on the sterile modern great room. The contrast between upstairs and down suggested the family had been in the middle of renovations. These inconsistencies in style—like the dining room table—gave the house a distinct character. Real people had lived here.

Until LaFontaine had cut them down with a chainsaw.

Anna noticed him staring down the hall. She squeezed his

hand.

"Don't ruin it now," she said. "The girls are right in here."

She pointed to the bedroom doorway closest to the stairs.

A pair of giggles chimed from within.

Weston felt a pinch in his chest. A smile twitched to life on his face. Those giggles sent Weston back home, where he often heard his daughters' huddled laughter come down the hall, sounding as if they were conspiring over a great big prank. They had that kind of relationship. Sisters and friends, always. Through fights and fits and jealous accusations. Always friends.

"It's okay," Anna said and held Weston's hand in both of hers. "They're waiting. They want to see their daddy so badly."

God, how easily he had swallowed the lie. The further he went along with it, the more it swept him away. If La-Fontaine wanted a broken and bereft man to kill, he had played the wrong hand.

Anna gave his arm another tug.

This time, Weston let her pull him along, across the threshold, and into the most beautiful dream he could have ever hoped for.

Callie and Coralee sat on the edge of a twin bed with a Sesame Street headboard, much of the paint rubbed off of Cookie Monster and Big Bird, marks of a long life. The rest of the room said all boy.

A radio controlled monster truck parked on the floor. A book shelf with clear plastic bins that held action figures and Matchbox cars and more Legos. A pile of dirty laundry tucked in one corner on the other side of tall dresser, as if the boy had stashed them there to keep from having to take them downstairs to the laundry room.

Weston had loved his girls, but he had sometimes wished

he could have had a boy, too. If for no other reason than that he could play with the toys and relive some of his own childhood through his son.

The girls were practically bouncing off the mattress as they looked up at Weston with wide smiles. One of Callie's front teeth was missing, just like it was the last time he saw her alive. Between the missing tooth, her freckles, and the red hair she got from her mother, she could very well have been the most adorable eight-year-old girl in history (in Weston's not-so-humble opinion).

And Coralee. At thirteen she was caught between the awkward cuteness of a child and the beginnings of a beautiful young woman. It filled Weston with pride while breaking his heart at the same time. She had her dark hair pulled back with a red elastic band.

Both of them wore long T-shirts as nighties. Callie's had Tweety Bird printed on hers. Coralee's featured some pop band that had gone out of style not long after...

Weston blinked the water out of his eyes. Tears ran down his cheeks. He opened his mouth, wanting to tell them how much he loved them, how much he missed them, but all that came out was a hollow mumbling, as if—

Oh, God. No.

He couldn't feel his tongue. It was... gone. He poked his fingers between his teeth. The tips touched the remaining stub at the back of his throat. It was like his tongue had been cut out of his mouth. Just like the Beast had done to Christopher.

Just like the Beast had done to his family.

As if on cue, the girls opened their jaws to reveal the damage the Beast had done. Without a tongue, the gap in Callie's teeth looked sadly obscene—an absence made in the process of growth contrasted against a gruesome absence made out of violence. Worse yet, Coralee smiled with her mouth agape, as if proud of her display.

Weston's scream sounded empty without his tongue, like a cry in a dark cave.

He fell to his knees, face wet, hands clenched in fists and pressed against the sides of his head.

How could he be so stupid?

Did he really think this would end any other way?

The girls closed their mouths and slid off the edge of the bed to their bare feet. They came to him, wrapped their arms around him. He was too horrified to pull away.

All he could do was weep while embraced by his dead daughters.

24

SADNESS FILLED LAFONTAINE'S EYES AS he came into the den and shut the door behind him, all the while keeping the gun on Kate.

The look irked her. If he was trying to garner sympathy just because she knew it wasn't him pulling all the strings here, he'd have better luck swallowing an alligator in one gulp.

He tilted his head toward the computer. "You found it?"

Kate looked down at the screen. The photo was gone. As was the file folder with her name on it.

"I'm not a tenth as powerful as my father," he said. "But I have a few tricks I can sneak past him." Then he frowned. "I was a little late with this one, I'm afraid."

"I don't understand." The wind found a gap in the window and sounded like a high-pitched dog whistle coming through. "Not one damn thing you've said since we met has made any sense."

His shoulders sagged. He sighed. "All along I've tried to keep you away from here. But whatever it is about this house, people like us can't seem to resist it."

"Like us, huh? Doesn't seem to bother you much."

"You're wrong. For as long as I have lived, this house has tugged at me like a lost memory." He strolled closer to the desk between them, keeping his aim on Kate. "I can't explain it all. I only know it's something my father discovered long before I was born."

"So... what?" Kate said. "He's your father, so you're obligated to help him? Give me a fucking break."

He made a face as if he had just stepped in shit. "Not because I want to. I don't have a choice."

Briefly, Kate thought of her own father. Mitch had been a complete ass right up to his death. Even so, while he struggled through his cancer, Kate took care of him. It's what you did with family. Call it duty or obligation or restitution. Whatever. Whether you liked them or not, family belonged to you, and it was up to you to take care of your own.

The comparison to LaFontaine's relationship with his own father was a big stretch, though. First off, Jacques LaFontaine was not sick, he was old. And if Kate was right about this, he was *very* old. A man his age still breathing was unnatural. The only reason he was alive was because he stole that life from others.

Which was another huge difference between her father and LaFontaine's. Mitch might have been a class-A jerk, but he wasn't a serial killer.

She shook her head. "You don't get to play the dutiful son card here."

He spat air. Made that stepped-in-shit face again. "I don't give a damn that he's my father. I don't have a choice because if I don't help him feed on others, he'll feed on me."

That was a nasty and pathetic twist. "You're killing... *brutally* killing families, husbands, wives, mothers, *children*. All just to save your own skin? And I'm supposed to feel sorry for you?"

"I never asked for sympathy."

"Yet you're still whining 'poor me' while you stand there pointing a gun at me."

"You think I want this? I told you back at the diner that the house would kill you, but you're the ones who insisted on coming anyway."

"How about this?" Kate said. "Drop the gun, get your daddy down here, and we'll all have a nice chat until the storm clears and the cops can come to put the two of you away for life. That would ease your conscience, wouldn't it?"

"I wish it were that simple."

"What's complicated about it?"

He let out a big, woe-is-me sigh. "You're not the only one who has lost someone."

"Another sob story? LaFontaine, you should know by now that those don't work on me. If I got a nickel every time I heard one from the losers I've arrested, I'd break the mint."

"My point," he said, "is that he can use that against me the same way he's doing it to you. Believe me, I've tried to tell him no, I've tried to leave..." He swallowed and winced as if it hurt. "I even tried to kill myself. But you've seen it. He can make them appear so real that they practically *are* real."

"Are you telling me he can control us?" Kate folded her arms. "Not buying it. He'd have us running around here like puppets if he could do that."

LaFontaine hung his head. He let the gun down a little. If the desk hadn't been in the way, Kate could have jumped him and disarmed him pretty easily at that moment.

He laughed softly.

"Don't you see?" he said. "He *has* had you running around like puppets."

The wind whistling from the window seemed to blow right through Kate, as if she were little more than air herself. Her whole body went cold. She wanted to argue with LaFontaine. But she couldn't.

Because he was right.

Kate pointed at the gun. "So what's that for? Where's your chainsaw?"

He'd gotten really good at looking like a guy with shit on his shoe. "Mr. Weston used the journal, I see."

She still had it in her pocket. She pulled it out and dropped it on the desk. The leather cover snapped against the desk's surface. "You fucked with him good with that thing."

"It was just a way of me trying to help you."

The laugh that buzzed in the corners of the room sounded so cynical, Kate didn't recognize it as her own. "Okay, LaFontaine. How are you going to help me now?"

"It's too late," he said. "Dad thinks you're too dangerous. A wild card. Which is the first time I ever heard him say that. Nothing scares him."

Kate enjoyed the feel of the smirk tugging her cheek. "But *I* do, huh?"

"I suppose so." He readjusted his hold on the Beretta, moving it higher on the grip. Then he raised his free hand and wrapped the other side of the grip like an experienced shooter. So hoping for a miss that would give her time enough to turn the tables on him didn't look promising.

"He doesn't want to fatten me up?" Kate asked. "He's sure about that?"

"He wants to. But my father hasn't lived for nearly two hundred years by being stupid."

"Two hundred years? How is that even possible without your little community here not noticing?"

"You just have to outlive everyone who remembers how old you are."

A bitter taste filled Kate's mouth. "None of the other guys in your little club are in on this?"

He shook his head. "They know he's really old. And he does still age after all. Just not as quickly, and with occasional bursts of... vitality."

"Bursts of vitality? How the hell does he explain that?"

"Diet. Exercise. Homeopathic remedies. He avoids being photographed, if he can help it, and the ones like that wedding picture get tucked away, a distant but pleasant memory. That bride was only one of several of his wives. Long before my time." He shrugged. "Like I said, no one really remembers how old he is. And whatever questions they have, for the most part they fill in the blanks themselves. I mean, what else are they going to think? That he's some kind of monster who feeds on people to keep him alive?"

Kate had seen it herself. When people were confronted with something they couldn't explain, they explained it away, rather than suspect the impossible.

The collar of her parka scratched her neck. It wasn't zipped tight, but it still felt like a noose.

"You're just gonna to shoot me," she said. "How anticlimatic."

"I'm sorry. In another life we might have been friends."

"Not even in an alternate universe, asshole."

LaFontaine raised the gun and lined up the sight on Kate.

25

THE PRESSURE OF HIS LITTLE GIRLS' bodies against Weston as they hugged him made his skin crawl instead of offering the comfort it normally would. He wanted to get to his feet, shove them away, curse them for the wicked lies they were. But his arms felt like rubber, his legs like jelly, and breathing had become difficult. It was as if...

...as if the energy was draining from his body.

Anna came over and knelt beside them.

Weston groaned at the thought that she might join in on the embrace. He would suffocate for sure. His family would kill him.

Thankfully, she kept her hands folded on her lap. She smiled at Weston. It still really looked like Anna's smile. The concerned expression mimicked hers perfectly—a look she would give him after a rough day at the mill, even while he insisted a bad day as the owner of the mill was nothing compared to one suffered by a work-a-day employee.

She never let him belittle his own troubles, though.

She had always been so supportive.

More tears welled in Weston's eyes. He welcomed them because they blurred his vision and saved him from seeing the false Anna so clearly.

Energy continued to leak out his body. If not for the girls holding him, he would have tipped over on his side.

Kate and Christopher had been right.

He eats them.

LaFontaine was eating him now.

Weston squeezed his eyes shut. Tried to will his grief and terror away. Those were the things that "fattened" him. If he could bury those emotions, he could make himself less... appetizing.

But the stifling warmth of his daughters' bodies pressed against him didn't go away when he closed his eyes. And the vision of their open and tongueless mouths was there to haunt him in the dark of his mind's eye.

A howl pushed through the phlegm clogging his throat. He noticed he could feel his full tongue again.

"Leave me alone."

The girls giggled and hugged him tighter.

He tried to get his arms to work. They twitched, but otherwise didn't respond. He felt as if he'd spent a whole day stacking lumber. A green nausea bubbled in his stomach. He could taste bile tainted with the remains of the BLT from the restaurant, which he so badly regretted finishing right now.

"Please," he moaned. "Get away from me."

Protests only pulled them closer. Their hair brushed his cheeks as they leaned their heads against the top of his.

Vertigo spun him like a barrel down a hill. Which made the nausea worse. He also felt himself drifting. It was that feeling you get when bobbing on the surface of sleep, but not quite sinking in.

He was on the verge of losing consciousness.

If he did, he knew he would never wake up again. La-Fontaine would finish his feast and then come in with his chainsaw to polish off his dessert.

At this point, he didn't care.

The darkness would take him away from the horrible touch of his daughters.

He'd been such a fool to fall for LaFontaine's trick. He should have known better. Should have seen the illusion as the bait it was.

Too late for regrets.

He broke the surface of consciousness.

And sank into the black.

26

"BACK UP AGAINST THE WALL." LaFontaine said.

Kate narrowed her gaze, keenly aware of the black eye of the Beretta staring back at her. "Why?"

LaFontaine jerked the gun. "Just do it."

His breathing was erratic. Sweat dampened his brow and some of the white curls just above. He looked close to suffering a panic attack.

Kate slowly backed away from the desk until she came against the wall to one side of the window. The wall felt cool, even through her parka. The blizzard battering the house was giving the heater a run for its money.

LaFontaine crept around the desk until he stood five feet in front of Kate. He had the gun aimed at center mass. A head shot was a more expedient execution, but he wasn't taking chances.

Unlike she had with him, LaFontaine wasn't underestimating Kate.

"Now stay there," he said.

"Where am I gonna go?"

"Shut up."

Kate's brow furrowed. "What's the problem, LaFontaine?"

He licked his lips. His eyes shone in the floor lamp's muted light. Nostrils flared.

"This up against the wall shit," Kate said. "You're just stalling."

He didn't say anything. Stood there. Frozen. Except for a small twitch under one eye.

Kate made a disgusted sound. "You can murder a whole family with a fucking chainsaw, but you can't bring yourself to put a single bullet in me?"

"What I did to them will haunt me forever."

"Again with the poor me bullshit."

His eyes watered. "I don't want to kill anymore."

Kate said nothing. She had nothing to say to this pathetic creep.

Inexplicably, LaFontaine inched forward. His aim trembled, but stayed true.

She bit back questioning him about what the hell he was doing now. She had a theory. And if she was right, she didn't want to risk breaking the spell.

"The things he's made me do," LaFontaine said. "I'll never find redemption. It's another reason I kept doing it. I am beyond forgiveness. Helping my father prolong his life was the only kindness I had left to give."

The twisted logic of a psychopath. Kate never got tired of the creative ways sickos justified their horrific actions. No. That wasn't true. She was damn sick of that bullshit. Killers didn't deserve any comfort, not even from their own twisted minds.

"Shoot me," she said, "so I don't have to listen to you whine anymore."

His lips puckered. The lines around his mouth aged him. His eyes flicked back and forth as if uncertain where to look.

Kate took a tentative step forward. Her own nerves jangled. This could end so easily. LaFontaine could rediscover his nerve in a second, pull the trigger in the next.

"Stop," he said, his voice thick.

Kate took another step forward, subtracting one of the five feet between them. The closer she moved toward the gun, the faster her heart beat. She thought about Christopher. If LaFontaine killed her now, she wouldn't be able to save the boy from this nightmare trap. But moving closer to death was her only option for escaping it.

"You don't want to kill me," she said. Her shaky breath curled around her words. Showing a little fear was good. It might resonate with LaFontaine's guilt. "Put the gun down."

"I can't," he said. "I can't put it down."

His finger curled around the trigger.

He's gonna do it, she thought.

Kate dodged left. LaFontaine spent his last reserve of hesitation, buying Kate enough time to get out of the gun's trajectory before he took the shot.

The gun blast rang in Kate's ear drums like a pair of bells. Hot gun powder singed her cheek. She ducked low and drove forward. Caught LaFontaine in the gut with her shoulder. Kept charging forward. Knocked LaFontaine off balance. Threw him down to the floor.

He landed with an *oof*. The gun sailed out of his grip and tumbled across the carpet.

Kate came down beside him. She jabbed him with an awkward left. Her knuckles struck his skull. Dull pain throbbed through her fingers. But she didn't stop there. She leaned up on her elbow and gave him another left. This time her fist punched him in the eye.

He cried out, his hands shooting up to cover his face. He rolled away.

He had nearly twenty years on her. His reaction time lagged behind Kate's by a large margin. She was up on her feet before he could push himself fully to his hands and knees. She kicked him in the ribs.

He grunted and flopped down on his belly. He laced his hands behind his head like they taught kids to do under their school desks in case of a natural disaster.

But if Kate was a natural disaster, she was a fucking tsunami and LaFontaine's house was made of straw.

She kicked him again and again, directing each blow to the same spot, until she had weakened him enough to stop struggling.

Panting, she backed away from his still body. She might have broken a couple of his ribs, but she couldn't have knocked him unconscious. He had given up. His only movement was the uneven hitch from his breathing, which probably hurt like a bitch from the punishment Kate had delivered to his side.

"Now," she said between gasps, "I might feel a little sorry for you."

She thought of Christopher again. Of the torture La-Fontaine's father was probably putting him through, using Lucy to cut into the boy's psyche like a butcher's blade, and opening him to relive the memory of the Beast's brutal attack.

Kate curled her lip. "Nope. Still not feeling it."

She kicked him one more time for Chris's sake.

27

THE DARKNESS IS A BEAUTIFUL THING.

Blinds you to the unforgiving world.

Deafens you to the haunting screams.

Numbs you to the pain.

Until the darkness turns against you, peeling back to expose you to the cruelty of nightmares and memories.

Weston sits at the dinner table. He can still smell the sawdust on his flannel shirt. The last fingers of daylight reach through the window above the kitchen sink. One of them touches Anna, making her red hair flare, painting her fair skin with its glow. She sits beside him at the round table. Steam rises from the plate in front of her. Butter chicken with a side of steamed peas.

Weston hates peas, and would prefer a baked potato, but they're trying to cut back on their sugar and starch. Which has proven its benefits, as Weston has taken to pulling his belt two notches tighter to keep his pants from dropping to his ankles. So he scoops some peas from his own plate with a fork and down the hatch they go. He can hold his breath to keep from tasting them, but he still has to suffer their mushy texture between his tongue and the roof of his mouth.

Anna stifles a smile, directing her gaze down on her plate. She looks like a middle-schooler who just left a tack on the teacher's chair.

The girls don't bother to hold back their laughter. Daddy's eating peas. Look at the face he's making. Poor Daddy.

Callie and Coralee have loved peas since they each started eating solid food. Weston can't understand it. Kids aren't supposed to like peas. But these two would scarf 'em down with every meal if they could.

It's a week away from Coralee's thirteenth birthday, and she can't stop talking about the party her mother is throwing for her. Or all the presents she's sure she'll get. Every day for the past month, she has reminded Anna and him both that she expects to get LMFAO's latest release.

Weston understands his daughter's taste in music even less than her love of peas.

Anna had to explain what LMFAO stood for, then assured him that she was on the same page and did not think the band was age appropriate for Coralee.

"All my friends listen to them," Coralee had immediately protested at the first sign of her mother's hesitation.

If they didn't get the album for her, they would surely hear that a thousand times more.

The price for being a parent. One Weston is perfectly willing to pay. When she's eighteen, she can listen to any-thing she wants.

After they've had their laugh, Weston's family eats quietly. Callie left the TV on in the living room as usual. Requests for her to turn it off when she was done watching stuck as good as soap on sheet metal. From the sounds of it, Rainbow Dash and Pinkie Pie are trying to solve whatever little problems little ponies have.

For some reason, on this average evening, Weston feels as if he hasn't seen his family in years. He can't stop stealing glances at the girls. Can't stop squeezing Anna's thigh under the table. His chest feels full of hot air and if he stepped outside, the spring breeze might carry him away.

His cheeks ache from smiling so much.

The taste of the peas don't even bother him so much.

He loves his ladies so much.

Then he hears a voice. Vaguely familiar, but from another, forgotten life.

Noah, you have to wake up.

Weston pauses with a bite of butter chicken on his fork and halfway to his mouth. The chicken should smell sweet from a hint of hickory, but it smells like ash instead. And the bite he just swallowed has left behind the taste of ash.

"What's wrong?" Anna asks. "Are the peas really that bad?"

"Did you hear something? A voice?"

Anna wrinkles her brow, but she's still smiling a little. "The TV is on," she says while giving Callie a pointed stare.

Callie sinks in her seat. "Sorry."

"No," Weston says. "It wasn't the TV."

But it had to be. Either that, or Weston is hearing voices in his head. He's pretty sure he isn't crazy. His life's too good. God has graced him with love and prosperity. There's nothing around to drive him crazy.

The girls are staring at him now. Daddy's acting weird. He's joking around. He's being a goof.

Anna sets down her fork, dabs her mouth with the red and white checkered napkin from her lap. "Stop being silly. The girls think you're serious."

"I…" *Am* is the next word on his lips until he holds it back. If he *is* hearing voices, he doesn't need to scare the girls over it. Besides, it was just the TV. Just the TV.

Noah, please. He's killing you.

Weston drops his fork. It clatters against his plate. Flecks of the sauce on the chicken spatters the checkered tablecloth that matches the napkins. A metallic flavored wetness rolls up the back of his throat. It tastes like blood.

"Daddy," Callie says with a quiver. "What happened to your mouth?"

He wipes his lips on the back of his hand. Leaves behind a red streak.

It reminds him of something, but he doesn't know what.

He's killing you. He's right there and he's…

…he's eating you.

The ladies in Weston's life all stare at him as if he has announced he has terminal cancer. Coralee's gaze hits hardest. She always looks so serious, even when she's smiling. She's not smiling now. None of them are.

Anna sparks into a fluster of motion. She drags her napkin through the air like a magician's handkerchief and wipes at Weston's mouth with a motherly touch, somehow both firm and gentle at the same time.

"It's okay," she says. "Daddy just bit his cheek. I guess we need to teach him how to chew."

The girls visibly relax, but their eyes still hold suspicion.

Weston takes the napkin from Anna to tend to himself. The blood isn't coming from his cheek. It's coming up his throat like a reverse trickle, gravity be damned.

You're almost dead, Noah.

Weston wonders if he does have cancer. A brain tumor. Maybe another on his lungs to explain the blood. The voice sounds like a child's. A boy about Coralee's age, maybe a little younger. But could it be the voice of God? If so, the Lord has chosen an odd way to call him to Heaven.

He suddenly feels lightheaded. It reminds him of when he donated blood during the blood drive at church. He felt especially queasy afterward. It took two cookies and a cup of juice before the nurse would let him leave the tent.

The girls look worried again.

They start to cry.

Their tears are blood.

Anna sobs. She, too, cries blood.

Weston jumps to his feet, knocking his chair over. "My God, what's happening?"

Anna tries to speak, but her mouth is full of blood. It runs down her chin as thick as motor oil.

He's about to scream when the voice in his head screams for him.

NOAH!

The darkness is a beautiful thing.

Until it turns against you.

Either you escape, or you become part of the black.

Weston finally recognizes Christopher's voice.

And he climbs his way out of the darkness, leaving behind its betrayal.

28

AFTER RECOVERING HER BERETTA, KATE hurried out of the den. She would rip this house apart until she found Christopher. Then she would find LaFontaine's father and do what he had kept nature from doing for well over a hundred years.

But she didn't have to rip apart the house. She nearly collided with Christopher as she came out of the foyer and into the great room. Kate shrieked as she came up short before knocking him over. His hoodie had dirty stains on the front and down the sleeves as if he'd been crawling around in a root cellar. Kate hadn't seen any sign of a cellar, though. Just the basement.

She took the boy's arm so he knew she was with him. "Are you okay?"

They had me locked in a room upstairs. But I got out.

They had him locked up? Kate felt like she could grind her teeth down to dust from clenching her jaw. The feel of her Beretta in her hand comforted her a little. Jacques La-Fontaine could play all the mind tricks he wanted. All she needed was one clear shot, then the nightmares he spun would stop for good.

Christopher took her hand and pulled.

We have to help Noah. They're killing him.

A fresh charge of adrenaline pumped through her system. Apparently, Jacques didn't need his son to do all the dirty work. The old man had probably been doing this long before Adrien was born, and was quite capable of slaughtering his victims without him.

"You know where he is?"

Christopher nodded.

Kate followed his lead. He took her through the house as easily as if he could see. And the confidence in his stride was beyond his eleven years. They headed toward the back of the house and ended up in the laundry room.

It felt like a million years ago since the last time she was in this room, though it couldn't have been much longer than an hour or so. She cringed internally, thinking the boy was about to say that Weston was down in the basement.

Instead, he guided her to the back door.

Kate drew back. "He's outside?"

The pole barn. They have him in there.

"Why in God's name would they drag him through that mess outside just to get him to a barn?"

I don't know. But I can sense where he is. I can lead you to him.

Let Chris back out into the blizzard? Hell no.

"I can't let you go out there," she said. "Especially not dressed the way you are."

I'm okay.

"Forget it." She wagged a finger at him even though she

knew he couldn't see it. "And don't you pull that 'I can make my own decisions' crap, 'cause it isn't gonna fly."

They're killing Noah.

"Then I'll have to get to him myself." She peered out the back window. The only light spilling into the laundry room still came from the dining room, so it was dim enough to see through the glass without a glare getting in the way.

But there might as well have been a glare. She couldn't see shit through all the blowing snow.

We have to hurry.

She could sense his panicked impatience. His relationship with Weston had the emotional equivalent of rebar holding it together. Kate couldn't imagine what losing Noah might do to the boy. The poor kid had suffered enough loss.

She wasn't sure how she would deal with losing him either. She didn't even want to entertain the thought.

He's almost dead. I can feel him fading.

Without waiting for a response, he wrenched the door open.

The wind plowed in like the thrust from a rocket. It pushed Kate off balance and teased her with a moment of vertigo. She stumbled, but kept her feet. The snow had turned into tiny shards that cut against her face like shattered crystal. She squinted into the arctic blast as the wind whipped her hair back.

We have to go. Now.

Kate let slip a frustrated growl. If the kid was this bull-headed at eleven, she hated to think what he'd be like as a teenager.

"Fine." She yanked down the zipper on her parka, tucked her gun in its holster, then shrugged the parka off. "But you're wearing this."

He backed away from her as if she was brandishing a

knife.

I can't.

"What do you mean you can't?"

Rather than answer, he took off into the storm.

She shouted after him, then yanked her parka back on, zipped up, and charged out after him.

He had only gone as far as the back porch, which felt like it might have been made of concrete or patio stones, but was impossible to tell under the seven or eight inches of snow. Despite the hardened flakes now swirling around them, the powder on the ground had some fluff to it. Kate's boots sank right through, and the snow swallowed her calves.

They hesitated on the edge of the porch, marked by a lattice archway. Snow clung to the lattice, but she could still see the dead vines woven through it. Otherwise, the snow hid where the porch ended and the yard began. She could barely see more than three feet in front of her. Christopher looked like a washed out mirage beside her. She couldn't believe the cold hadn't brought him to his knees dressed the way he was.

In fact, he didn't so much as tremble.

Meanwhile, Kate's teeth had already started to ache from chattering. Her lungs cried out in cold pain with every inhale. The air tasted like sheet metal.

She yanked her stocking cap out of her pocket and pulled it down over her ears. Still didn't have any damn gloves, though. Her fingers quickly went stiff, and the skin on the backs of her hands stung.

Christopher reached out to her while he stared out away from the house, as if, despite his blindness, he could see through the white gales and dark night.

Kate took his hand. It felt impossibly warm.

The hairs on the back of her neck stood on end. Her primal instincts were trying to tell her something.

Christopher didn't give her a chance to listen. He pulled her by the hand through the lattice archway and into oblivion.

29

IN THE MIDDLE OF A raging blizzard, the wind scattered time as much as it did snow. Kate lost track of how long they wandered in the whitewashed night. Probably not long. It felt both like a blink and an eternity.

Every step through the snow became a labor twice as hard as the last. Her leg muscles burned. And she did sweat, but the moisture cooled as quickly as it flowed, never giving her a chance to enjoy any body heat.

As miserable as she felt, Christopher kept trudging along at the same pace. A few times it felt as if he was going to yank her arm out of its socket. She couldn't seem to go fast enough for his tastes.

She didn't know if it was an adrenaline overdose that lent him his strength, the kind that powered the proverbial mother who lifts a car off of her pinned child, or if Kate's own adrenaline had peaked out during her confrontation with LaFontaine, and now she was crashing.

Whatever the case, they had wandered too long. Kate recalled the pole barn from when they had first pulled up to the house, and felt confident that, based on her estimate of the distance between the buildings, they should have reached it by now.

"Christopher," she shouted into the wind. The wind easily overwhelmed her voice. "We're lost."

She dug her heels in—easy to do in the deep snow—and held fast while the boy tried to drag her along.

When she didn't give in, Christopher snapped his head around to look over his shoulder at her. And that was just it. She felt like he could actually see her, like he wasn't blind at all.

His lips peeled back from his teeth. The wind whipped his hood off. The sweat in his hair instantly turned to frost.

He let go of her hand.

"Can't keep up?" he asked. Not in her head, but aloud. Impossible without his tongue. More impossible—his voice belonged to Kate's mother. "Poor, Kate. All lost in the snow."

Kate staggered backward. With her legs nearly buried to her knees, backing up didn't work so well. Her feet caught and she fell on her ass. A wet chill penetrated her jeans. She had thrown her hands back to break her fall. Now they disappeared into the snow, and her bare skin cried out as if burnt, not frozen.

A white dervish swirled around Christopher, obscuring him completely from sight. When his silhouette reemerged, it had changed.

Kate's mother strolled over to her, her feet on top of the snow as if she were too light to sink in.

Of course she was. Mental projections carried no weight.

Jacques LaFontaine had duped Kate, and good. She

screamed, not out of fear this time, but a boiling rage the harsh wind couldn't cool. "You son of a bitch."

Her mother drew close enough for Kate to make out more of her features, including her crooked smile. The wind and blowing snow seemed to split around her as if she stood in an invisible bubble. Now the stifled moonlight made her easy to see. Her smile turned into a sneer.

"Did you really think you could get the better of me?" she asked, her voice distorted, sounding like the creak of a rotten floorboard. "I'm in your head, Kate. As difficult as you are, not even you can fight your own mind."

Kate screamed again. She tried to get to her feet, had to work at it. The snow wanted to bring her down, embrace her, bury her. But she was stronger than snow. And she was stronger than Old Man LaFontaine gave her credit for. Once she finally stood, she shook the icy powder off her hands. The flakes were so frozen, they fell away like dust, leaving her skin almost dry. What moisture stayed behind had already turned to frost, fused to her knuckles, the backs of her hands, and in the creases in her palms.

Frost bite was inevitable. She just hoped she could get out of the storm before she lost her hands completely.

"The nice thing is," her mother said, "I can still feed on you out here as the storm kills you. It won't be much. Nothing like what I'm getting from the one I'm draining right now. Your gentleman friend. But when you're as old as I am, you take what you can get."

"No," Kate growled through her teeth.

She turned away from her mother, tucked her hands in her pockets for what little protection that would provide, and started to trudge forward. Five labored steps through the increasing accumulation, and her mother materialized in view through the white mist.

"You can't run away from me, Kit Kat." She went to touch Kate's face. Kate flinched out of reach. "I'll be with you until you die."

Fine. Let this fabrication tag along. Kate had to focus on finding her way either to the barn or back to the house. The problem was, every direction looked the same, an ashen haze of nothingness.

Kate decided forward was as good as any trajectory. She lurched ahead, walking right through the illusion of her mother. These things were nothing but vapor if you didn't let yourself be seduced by them.

Of course, her mother reappeared ahead, standing to one side of her path like a street sign.

"Keep going, Kate. Walk yourself into hypothermia. Wear yourself out. Drop to your death."

Kate stopped. She screwed up her face against the slicing snow. She eyeballed her mother, then made a decision.

Kate turned right, and started heading in that direction.

Her mother faded behind her and didn't show up again for about twenty feet. Again, off to Kate's right.

"That's it. I can feel you weakening."

Kate turned left.

Ten more steps, and there her mother was, standing off to one side like a spectator cheering on a marathon runner. She looked radiant, untouched by the storm. So much color in her face, her hair back in its braid, her head tilted with adoration in her eyes.

The old man liked to tease. Turn her mother into an enemy, then back to her loving self. Kate wondered if he really needed to inflict this cruelty to fatten his psychic meal, or if it was a fetish, something he did because he could, the closest thing to a hand job a two hundred-year-old wack job could get.

Kate turned left again, ignoring the cramps in her legs and the ice in her joints. She could feel the energy seeping from her body. Not just exhausted. The old man was chewing his food.

This time, Kate barely took three steps before her dear, fake mother popped up directly in front of her.

She practically glowed. Except for her face. Frost bite had peeled away her skin. Ragged patches with crisp, icy edges on her forehead, one cheek, her chin, around one eye. The frost bite had eaten through the spot on her cheek so that Kate could see her mother's teeth and part of her jaw bone underneath.

Among all this damage, her mother grinned.

"That's it, Kate. Keep going."

And she did. Once again passing through her mother, who broke apart and became part of the whirling snowfall.

Three steps.

Her mother stood in front of her once more. A flap of skin hung off her forehead over her eye. "Why are you bothering?" she asked. "Give up and die already."

Kate could barely feel a thing anymore, as if she had left her body somewhere behind her, and only her soul pressed on. But she still managed a stiff smirk.

Jacques had tipped his hand.

Nothing deterred Kate anymore. No matter how many times her mother materialized in front of her, Kate stayed on course. Eventually, her mother stopped appearing at all. And shortly after that, Kate made out a wide shadow ahead. The shadow grew to an angular silhouette, until finally she could see the corrugated metal flank of the pole barn.

She wasn't sure if she had wandered out of the old man's range (which seemed unlikely considering how far he had reached to bring them here) or if he'd given up. Kate found her way into the barn through a side door without any more interference. She slammed the door shut and fell to the concrete floor, gasping. Each breath felt like steel wool all the way down into her frozen lungs.

The smell of motor oil and something putrid hung in the air.

There was nothing warm about the barn. Kate's breath streamed out of her mouth and nose in thin clouds. Every inch of her trembled. Her hands had turned to icy claws in her pockets. But she was out of the wind. Away from the snow.

Away from Christopher, too.

Kate's mother might as well have directed Kate into a prison cell.

Laying on a concrete slab, bemoaning her situation, wouldn't help any. She gathered her strength and stood.

Like a gift, she saw it before her, by the barn's large sliding door. She had forgotten LaFontaine mentioning it.

His snowmobile.

30

WESTON OPENED HIS EYES, BUT the vision of his family around the dinner table, the blood pouring from their mouths, stayed imprinted like a double exposure across the room.

He blinked a few times. The vision faded. His surroundings came into focus.

He was still in the bedroom that Anna had led him to. He lay curled up on his side, cheek pressed against the carpet, the nap scratchy against his stubble. The scent of carpet freshener still clung to the floor, but faded, the ghost of a smell. He tasted blood. But it wasn't coming up his throat. The raw pain on the inside of his cheek told him he had chomped himself pretty good. And judging from the ache in his jaw, his teeth had been clamped hard while he suffered his dream.

Weston raised his head. It took way too much effort. His head was a wrecking ball, his neck the chain.

The ceiling light blared down on him, which made him feel like he was on an operating table. His eyes adjusted quickly enough.

The girls were gone. Anna was gone.

On the edge of the bed sat an old man. Weston knew he recognized the man, but he was out of context, didn't belong in this place, and didn't quite look as Weston remembered him.

LaFontaine had taken his father home from the restaurant and put him to bed.

So, why was he here?

And why did he look a little younger?

No... not really younger, but more invigorated somehow. More powerful. He was still hovering around ninety—no question there—but it was the best ninety Weston had ever seen. His eyes seemed clearer and more focused, his frame less fragile. He sat straight, the tired hunch to his shoulders gone.

The old man smiled. His teeth didn't look so yellow anymore.

Truth be told, Weston felt older than the man sitting on the bed.

He's eating you.

Weston couldn't tell if that was a memory of Christopher's voice, or if the boy was communicating with him now. His brain felt like a wet rag wrung dry. Confusion and dizziness was the new norm. But the meaning behind the words was clear enough. It wasn't LaFontaine feeding on their psychically amplified terror, it was his *father*, and it was rejuvenating him somehow. Keeping him alive beyond his natural years.

The old man had his hands folded in his lap. If a child had lain in the bed, the scene would have looked like grandpa

poised to start a bedtime story. "You, young man, are ripe."
He said *ripe* as if the word had a holy meaning, a super-
powered *hallelujah*.

Weston tried to speak. His mouth was numb and his
tongue fat, which made it too hard to put together a word, let
alone a sentence.

But at least he had a tongue.

"Hush, now. I'll bring your family back to comfort you
until it's time to finish." He leaned forward. The bed springs
creaked. "I didn't know one man could hold so much grief
without killing himself."

The old man cackled and clapped his hands together and
shook them as if he were about to unwrap a birthday present.
Weston wondered how many birthdays this man had really
seen.

"You three are so very different. Not even the early Stokers had this kind of power. And the boy..." He drifted off,
inhaled deeply through his nose, his eyes rolling back in his
head. "He's almost as strong as I am. I could feed off him for
a week or more."

He hooted and clapped his hands again. The snap echoed
in the quiet room.

Weston tried to prop himself up on an elbow. He got there,
but his arm jellied and he dropped back down on his side.

"I'm sorry," the old man said. "I promised you your family back."

His face went slack. He closed his eyes. His chest expanded and relaxed as he took long, deep breaths. His shoulders
drooped. His hands fell limp to his sides. Weston got the
sense that the old man wasn't there anymore.

"Oh, Noah." Anna came into view and laid down beside
him, her face inches away from his. She ran her hand
through his hair. "My poor guy. You've had a terrible day. I

swear that mill is going to give you an ulcer. Or worse."

Weston moaned. Anna's hand felt cool against his feverish head. His scalp tingled pleasantly with each stroke. He was too weak to fight the lie. If he had to die tonight, why bother?

Noah, you have to fight.

Christopher's voice felt like a thin needle in his brain. He grunted. Tried to go back to enjoying Anna's touch.

You're falling for it again. That's not Anna.

The old man hiccuped with his whole body. He bobbed on the mattress as the springs reacted to his sudden jerk. His serene face crinkled, as if suffering from bad gas.

Anna's mouth opened. She held still for a moment, her body rigid. Then she relaxed and went back to stroking his hair. "Stay with me, my guy. We deserve this time."

"Yeah, Daddy. Don't you want to come home with us?"

Coralee knelt by his head. She bent down and kissed Weston's cheek. Her lips felt like rose petals. She smelled like that baby shampoo he would wash her hair with in the bath, back when she was Callie's age. She was a teenager now, though barely. But to her mind, she was a woman, and dads weren't supposed to see their grown-up daughters without clothes. Besides, she didn't take baths anymore. She took showers.

She still used the baby shampoo, though.

You can't. Kate needs you. I need you. We're your family now. Your real family. Your living *family.*

Weston had never heard such desperate pain in Christopher's voice. It stirred something inside of him. An instinct he hadn't used in a long time. A fatherly instinct. Triggered by Chris. Not the imaginary family torturing him now.

A fresh wave of strength cycled through him. Then he felt a push, a jab to his mind, that scattered the fog. It was

Christopher. The boy was lending his own strength to Weston.

We need you, Noah.

And Weston needed them.

He rolled onto his belly, then pushed himself up on his hands and knees.

"Daddy, you're going to hurt yourself."

Callie had joined them. She stood by the dresser, hand over her mouth, eyes wide and worried.

He ignored her. He struggled to his feet. The room spun. Then he felt Christopher's psychic touch and the room settled. Clarity continued to wash his mind.

The old man twitched. His lower lip quivered. He brought his hands into his lap and worked them together as if fighting off the cold.

Weston pulled his lips back in what he meant as a grin, but felt more like a crazy scowl. He glared at the old man. "Chris just might have you beat."

The old man's eyes shot open. They were glazed with white. Like Christopher's blind eyes.

The image of Weston's wife and daughters began to flicker like a TV with bad reception. Anna's face contorted, features melting like hot wax, then reforming. Her nose grew out of her cheek. One eye dropped to just above her mouth. Her throat expanded like a fleshy bubble.

Similar mutations spread to his daughters. He could see the changes from the corners of his eyes. He refused to turn and look. Watching that horrific transformation would only fuel the old man's power, causing Christopher's efforts to backfire. He stopped looking at Anna, too. He pointed his gaze out the door. He had to get out of there. Legs still unsteady, he staggered toward the doorway.

Until the old man's son stepped in the way. One of his

eyes was red and swollen, his face fixed in a wince. And as LaFontaine blocked the exit, Weston felt something crack in his mind, even heard a sound, like the one his pencil made when he had snapped it in half. He lost the sense of Christopher within him. When he called out to him, he got no response.

"Beat by a little boy?" the old man asked from behind him. "Not fucking likely."

As if the old man had given a cue, Adrien LaFontaine moved forward, driving Weston back. Weston glanced over his shoulder to keep from tripping over something. He noted the images of his family had mercifully disappeared. But the weakness had returned and he didn't need anything to trip on. His legs gave out and he slammed to the floor, knocking his head on the bed frame.

The knock to the head stunned him. He didn't notice LaFontaine's approach until the white-haired man stood over him. He was holding something else Weston hadn't noticed before.

A hacksaw.

LaFontaine's lips were pressed together, the color around his mouth drained to white. His nostrils flared, but he didn't look angry. He looked scared.

"I'm sorry, Dad," he said while he kept his eyes on Weston. "The woman got the best of me."

"You got the best of you, you fucking coward." The old man's voice carried a liquid growl. "Never mind her. She's out in the storm."

Kate. How had he gotten her outside?

Dumb question. Between LaFontaine and his father, the three of them never stood a chance against their manipulation.

That didn't stop Weston from feigning bravado. "I'll kill

you both if you hurt my friends."

The old man snickered. "Cut him up, Adrien. I need to finish this meal before it spoils."

LaFontaine knelt beside Weston, pinned his arm to the floor.

Weston was too drained to resist.

"I'm so sorry," LaFontaine said. "I tried to warn you."

He raised the hacksaw.

Anna and the girls stood behind him, looking down at Weston with naked pity.

"We love you, Daddy," little Callie said, her red hair in pigtails. Instead of the big Tweety Bird T-shirt, she wore a plaid dress, white socks with ruffles around her ankles, and patent leather loafers. It was the outfit she had worn when Weston had dropped her off for her first day of second grade.

"We love you," Coralee echoed. She had a different T-shirt on with another boy band that resembled all the rest. She had it tucked into her black jeans in front, but left the back hanging out.

"See you soon, love," Anna said.

Then LaFontaine got to cutting.

31

THE SMELL OF GAS FILLED Kate's nose as she accelerated the snowmobile, cutting through the blizzard, blind as all hell, with the icy flakes stinging her cheeks. She had to keep her eyes closed to slits to prevent the snow from blowing in them, though she might as well have closed them—it was just a choice between all white or all black.

Kate remembered the general position of the house in relation to the barn. As long as she stayed straight, she would run right into the house. Hopefully only figuratively.

Eventually she saw its outline through the storm. She adjusted her trajectory toward where she thought the back door was located. She caught sight of a muted square of light framed by the window in the door.

Damn, I'm good.

The inflation to her ego lost all its air when the snowmobile's front skis grated against the edge of the porch. She couldn't see the lattice arch, but felt it break apart around her. A cracked edge cut her cheek. The cry of the metal skis against the stone porch made the sound of a fork against a chalkboard seem practically musical in comparison.

Kate had only a second for the noise to make her skin cringe, then she was flying forward, over the handle bars, twisting in the air. She flopped flat on her back in a snowdrift piled up against the house. It was the first—and probably only—time she was thankful for the snow.

The drift cushioned her fall, but she still got the wind knocked out of her. She had to take a second to catch her breath. The blizzard gathered more of the damned white stuff around her, threatening to make her part of the drift. She got to her feet, brushed snow off. She reached under her parka to check that her pistol was still secure in its holster.

It was.

Then she high-stepped it to the door and got her ass in the house.

Once inside, she dropped on her knees by the closest heating vent right next to the dryer. She put her hands flat against the floor grate. The metal felt hot against her skin. She didn't care. She was halfway tempted to light her hands on fire over the stove in desperation to thaw her knuckles.

She hated to take the time at the vent, but if she wanted to use her gun, she needed use of her fingers.

After a minute, she flexed and relaxed her hands several times to test their functionality. They moved. Still stiff.

Good enough.

She pulled her weapon and rushed out of the laundry room. Through the breakfast nook—the bear right in its original pose against the toy tank, not picked apart by the illusion of her mother. As she sailed by, she thought about the old man's impostor Christopher refusing to wear her parka.

I can't.

Of course he couldn't. The illusions might have had the power to make you *think* they were touching you, but they couldn't really touch anything. Including the things around them.

A minor and obvious thought. Yet it felt important.

She ran through the kitchen and charged into the open space between the island and the dining room. The shadows in the great room looked sharper, the corners cast by the furniture more pointed. Either another illusion or, more likely, her own imagination.

Once she stood in the center of the room, behind the austere sofa facing the fireplace, she pulled to a sudden halt.

Where was she going?

Upstairs?

Or should she head back to the basement?

Panic and adrenaline had her running without direction. She racked her brain, trying to remember if her mother had given her any clues as to where the LaFontaines were holding Christopher or Weston. But all she had said was that the old man was draining Weston right at that moment.

The basement felt right. It made sense. She started back in that direction.

But a scream froze her.

It came from upstairs.

Weston.

Her instincts had been right in the first place.

She adjusted her grip on the pistol to make sure she could fire the thing. Both hands throbbed and burned. Patches of her skin looked a little gray and were the only spots that didn't hurt. But she could curl her fingers around the pistol's grip, and she could move them well enough to pull the trigger.

Kate booked it into the foyer and up the stairs.
The screaming had stopped.
Which worried her more.

32

LAFONTAINE DRAGGED THE HACKSAW'S SERRATED blade across the top of Weston's wrist four times—twice forward, twice back.

The way the saw's teeth tugged his breaking skin like ripped fabric was a sickening sensation almost worse than the pain. Weston cried out, spittle and blood from the tear inside his cheek sprayed a mist and rained down on his face. The hot, liquid ooze spreading on his wrist clued him in to how deep the cut went, but he couldn't bring himself to look at it.

Any second now, LaFontaine would reach bone.

The old man cackled from his place on the bed, looming above like a king on a throne enjoying a bloody joust.

But only four swipes.

Then LaFontaine stopped.

He looked up from his work, across the room, eyes growing wide, mouth falling open. His breath caught. A soft and quivering whine came out from deep in his throat.

"Rebecca," he said, his voice like a breeze. "Rebecca."

"What are you doing?" his father said. From the creaky annoyance in his tone, Weston half expected his next words would be, *Get off my lawn.*

"What are you looking at?" he asked instead. He turned his eyes toward where LaFontaine stared. His face turned sour. *More* sour. "What the hell are you looking at?"

LaFontaine nodded. Probably not the response his father was looking for. "I know," he whispered. "So very long."

The saw blade still rested in the groove LaFontaine had cut in Weston's wrist. The metal felt so unnatural sunken into him like that, a metallic insult to his flesh. The blood pattered onto the carpet in a slow, uneven rhythm. Weston could smell his own sweat, a bitter and salty mix that turned his stomach.

Pain shot up his arm in waves, each wave reaching farther until he felt a twinge in his chest like the first signs of a heart attack.

"Who are you talking to?" the old man demanded.

LaFontaine's lips twitched as if it couldn't make up its mind to smile or scowl. Glimpses of his straight, bright teeth came and went.

"You can't see her?" he asked with a cross between wonder and hate. "You're the one putting her in my head again."

The old man snapped his gaze back to his son. "There's nobody there, you louse." The skin around his eyes gathered in, giving him the small-eyed glare of a T. rex. "You're letting him spoil."

LaFontaine's lips chose a form. Not just a scowl. The full-on, peeled back, teeth-baring grin of a rabid hound. He never turned away from whatever he saw beyond Weston's line of sight, somewhere above his head.

"It's Becca, Dad. You remember Becca."

"There's nobody there." The old man had a little doubt in his voice, a little frightened quiver. "*Nobody*."

"She's right there," LaFontaine said. As ugly as his rabid grin was, his words sighed out in a breathy whisper. His angry mouth was for his father, but everything else belonged to this Becca. His gaze. His voice. His breath. "She's right there, Dad. As beautiful as the day you killed her."

"You're hallucinating." But he looked back as if checking in case someone *was* there. "Get a hold of yourself. What in the Lord's name is wrong with you?"

Weston had been so consumed by his pain, and now La-Fontaine's strange behavior, he had forgotten about Anna and the girls. They still stood behind LaFontaine, but they weren't looking at Weston. They were looking across the room, same as the old man. Their expressions as angry and confused.

The old man kept the visions up, but apparently his preoccupied mind could no longer manipulate them.

"She's right there," LaFontaine said. "She hasn't aged a day."

"That's because she's not real. Something is tricking you. Can't you see that?"

Finally, LaFontaine lifted the saw from Weston's wrist. The edges of the wound clung to the blade for an instant, as if his flesh didn't want to let it go. That small tug woke up a whole new level of pain. His chest clenched. Tears rolled down his cheeks.

He focused on Anna. But not the ghost that stood in the room. He conjured up his own image of her. An image with no agenda. A vision he could trust. Her beautiful red hair. Her kind smile. The way her delicate fingers covered her mouth when she laughed.

The pain didn't give way. But Weston could bear it. It was just a scratch compared to the cut LaFontaine's father had inflicted by exploiting Weston's memory of his family, and twisting that memory against him.

It was time Weston took back ownership of those memories.

LaFontaine straightened his back. He held the saw up high enough that Weston could see his blood painted on the blade. But LaFontaine had forgotten all about Weston. He might as well have been part of the floor.

"She's *mine*," LaFontaine said, waggling his head and pinching his voice in sarcastic imitation. It sounded nothing like his father, but it didn't take a leap to figure out who he was quoting. "That girl belong to *me*."

"Shut up," his father said. "That little bitch helped keep me alive. Your *father*. Your flesh and—"

"You shut up!" White foam collected in the corners of LaFontaine's mouth. "I loved her. She was only sixteen. We were kids. And you killed her so you could add a few more years to your pathetic life."

For the first time, LaFontaine turned his attention away from across the room and aimed his gaze at his father. He brandished the saw as if he meant to throw it, his back arched, saw high above his head. He opened his mouth to say something more.

The gunshot silenced him.

He pitched forward, falling on top of Weston. He didn't land anywhere near the injured wrist, but the impact sent a jolt of pain through Weston anyway.

The saw tumbled from LaFontaine's grip, cartwheeled across the floor, and thumped to a stop four feet away. Tiny splotches of Weston's blood stained the carpet in the saw's wake.

LaFontaine turned to dead weight across him, making it a little harder to breathe. But his fall cleared the way for Weston to see past him.

Anna, Callie, and Coralee had vanished.

Kate stood in their place, a wisp of smoke curling away from the barrel of her gun.

33

JACQUES LAFONTAINE LAUNCHED TO HIS feet, a phlegmy gurgle in his throat as he cried out.

The sound plucked Kate's nerves. She spun toward the sound, raised her gun.

The old man's eyes bugged. His jaw opened and closed. He held out his bony hands as if to grab Kate by the throat. He looked to Kate like a mad scientist from an old 50's sci-fi flick. Only, off screen, the image was frightening instead of laughable. The air seemed to fill with an electric charge. The hairs on the nape of Kate's neck stood on end. The chill down her spine felt like the touch of a corpse's finger.

The old man didn't pay any attention to the pistol aimed at his chest.

After his attack on Weston, Jacques's body had grown stronger, full of vitality. But now he transformed in front of Kate. The taut skin began to slacken. His clear blue eyes turned milky and bloodshot.

In a matter of seconds, that vitality had vanished, returning him to the doddering old man they had met in the restaurant.

Kate had time to gasp before the world around her changed.

She stood at the mouth of an alley, which she recognized right away. The alley behind Sandy Point Mall, where her mother was found murdered. From where she stood, she could see the blue metal door with the bulb above it, its light creating a pocket in the night. On the other side of the door, a pair of Dumpsters with their lids propped open with empty boxes and plastic trash bags.

Between those bins, the Beast had left her mother's bruised and broken body.

Kate had never physically been in this alley, knew it only by crime scene photos and one other time.

A time like this. Almost exactly.

Back when she had first met Christopher in Santa Flora, she had sat down with him in her office. He held that pink photo album with *Lucy* scrawled across the cover. He gripped that thing as if his life depended on it. But then he offered it to her. And just like Weston's experience with LaFontaine's journal, Kate had been transported.

To this alley.

Back then, Kate had ridden in the mind of her mother's killer, seeing from his point of view as he walked down the alley to finish with his kill.

She did the same now.

When she looked down, she saw a man's hand—the Beast's hand—as he unhooked a flashlight clipped to his belt. She could also glimpse the security guard uniform he wore with the plastic name badge pinned to his shirt pocket, M. BONNER printed on its face—an alias he'd used for a period of time.

Kate realized that the old man had thrust her into a memory of a vision. She was reliving what Christopher had shown her through the album. A sickening déjà vu.

And while stuck in this vision, she couldn't turn away as the Beast reached the gap between the Dumpsters, the stink of garbage and fresh death on the chilly breeze.

With his flashlight on, the Beast crouched before her mother, and so did Kate. No choice in the matter. Just like last time.

There she lay in the flashlight's glare, her mother's limp body propped against the wall. Hair a mess. Face beaten beyond recognition. Her dead eyes caught the light and glistened as if she were crying.

When Christopher did this for Kate, he had meant for it, no matter how painful, to bring them closer together, to give Kate an understanding of his and Weston's quest to hunt the Beast and put him down.

That Jacques was now using that memory against her felt like blasphemy, and angered her to the core.

But her anger couldn't break the spell.

She had to watch—again—as the Beast drew his utility knife and opened its blade. She had to watch—again—as he stuck his fingers into her mother's mouth and pulled her tongue out. Watch—again—as he moved to cut her tongue with his blade.

Thankfully, this was the point where the other security guard interrupted Bonner before he could go through with his wicked surgery.

Kate anticipated the other guard's voice:

Hey, Mickey, what the hell is taking you so...

But it didn't come.

The elder LaFontaine had taken it upon himself to revise

history.

Now Kate had to watch the Beast complete his mutilation.

She wanted to scream. But Bonner didn't scream, so she couldn't. She wanted to cry. But Bonner probably didn't know the meaning of tears, except for those he saw in the eyes of his victims. So she couldn't cry. Having to silently watch wasn't the worst of it, though. Because she was *inside* the Beast. For the duration of this nightmare, she *was* the Beast. She could see what he saw. She could smell what he smelled.

And she could *feel* what he felt.

So she felt what it was like to cut out her mother's tongue.

Kate wanted to throw up. But the Beast's stomach was empty and undisturbed.

So she couldn't.

34

WESTON COULDN'T TELL FOR SURE where Kate had shot LaFontaine, but with his parka unzipped, and based on the warm wetness soaking through his sweater, LaFontaine was bleeding pretty good.

Right after Kate had fired, the old man popped off the bed like some gnarled imitation of a jack-in-the-box. The bed-springs yipped behind him.

Kate pivoted toward him, bringing around her gun.

The old man's face took on the wild-eyed grimace of a rubber Halloween mask. He reached his arms out, his fingers splayed crookedly. It reminded Weston of a bit from one of the Star Wars movies he'd caught on TV some random and bored evening after putting the girls to bed. A shriveled, gray man in a dark hood and robe gleefully shot lightning from his fingertips, red eyes staring at the guy writhing on the floor, taking the brunt of the crackling assault.

But this wasn't a movie. And the old man didn't need

lightning.

Kate's eyes shot wide for a second. Then they rolled back in her head, eyelids fluttering. Her body went slack, and the pistol slipped out of her hands and landed on the carpet with a *thump*.

The old man had her. Had her deep.

His complete focus on Kate, however, set Weston free from his own psychic trap. He could already feel some strength returning. He gritted his teeth against the burning pain around his wrist—which felt like a metal cuff fresh out of a blacksmith's forge—and shoved at LaFontaine's body with his good hand. LaFontaine rolled off and flopped face first between Weston and the bed.

When he landed, he let out a muffled *umph*. So he wasn't dead.

At least, not yet.

Meanwhile, Kate walked backward until she came against the wall. Her mouth hung open. Saliva glossed her lower lip.

Weston reached under LaFontaine's neck, worked his skinny tie loose, and yanked it off over his head, not at all concerned about being gentle. He lassoed the tie's loop around his injured arm, about six inches above the wrist, and wrenched it as tightly as he could. Then he wrapped the tail of the tie around and tucked the end in. He could feel his pulse throb against the makeshift tourniquet. The gush of blood from the jagged cut on the back of his wrist eased, but plenty continued to dribble over his knuckles and down his forearm.

LaFontaine groaned.

Cradling his arm, Weston staggered to his feet.

The gun lay a couple of feet on the other side of La-Fontaine.

The old man's piercing glare didn't so much as twitch. He

had his lips peeled back. His teeth had returned to their usual shade of yellow. The son of a bitch was reverting to his old self right before Weston's eyes. In fact, he looked even worse than before. Whatever he was doing to Kate, it was pulling on a whole lot of his stolen life-force.

Weston stepped over LaFontaine, reached down to grab the gun. He deplored these weapons, but had learned to shoot as a boy growing up in North Carolina, and sometimes you just had to do what needed to be—

Stopstopstopstaaaaaahp!

Christopher's sudden mental shouting made Weston start as if hit with the paddles of a defibrillator.

Don't. Kill. No.

It didn't matter that Christopher was only eleven years old. Weston would trust the boy with his life. But every muscle in his body wanted to ignore Christopher's panicked message.

Why shouldn't he kill the old man? He was probably killing Kate. And they knew he had, with the help of his son, killed many others.

It wasn't a moral dilemma. Weston had every right to put this man down. Kate would have approved of this sudden change of heart.

You'll kill Kate, too.

Weston drew away from the gun as if something had bit his hand. The swollen *thump thump* under his tourniquet picked up speed along with his heart rate. He shuffled back and almost tripped over LaFontaine.

He didn't have to ask for an explanation from Christopher. On an instinctive level, he understood the threat exactly. The old man was so deep into Kate's mind, if his brain suddenly stopped working, it might do permanent damage to Kate as well. It sounded a little ridiculous, but Weston knew in his gut it was true.

The little boy's bedroom seemed smaller. Closer walls. Less space between the furniture. The static-smelling air more stifling.

You have to come get me.

Between LaFontaine's tacky blood pasting Weston's sweater to his chest, and the sweat running down his back and sides, he couldn't stand the weight of his parka anymore. He whipped it off as if it meant to swallow him whole, and tossed it aside.

Where are you? he asked Christopher.

A room at the end of the hall. I'm locked in.

Weston gave the old man one last, longing glance—so desperate to see him dead—then rushed out of the room into the hallway.

The door at the end of the hall looked different than when he had first glimpsed it. The red looked a shade lighter, the color of blood.

He barreled down the hall. The sudden burst of physical strain increased the flow of blood running over the back of his hand. He did his best to ignore it.

He reared back and kicked the door.

The door held.

Weston, on the other hand, lost his balance and hit the floor, luckily using his good hand to break the fall.

Son of a bitch.

Using the wall for support, he pulled himself back to his feet.

The key is on the ledge above the door.

Weston glanced up, saw a glint of metal on top of the doorframe. "Now you tell me."

He reached up and grabbed the key. His hand shook a little when he tried to work the key into the lock, the *tic-tac* sound like the last rattles of a roulette ball. Finally, he jammed it home and turned it.

He cranked the knob and shoved the door open with his elbow. The hinges groaned, but the door easily swung wide.

The room had a bare hardwood floor covered with dust and in desperate need of resurfacing. Cardboard boxes were stacked in all four corners, making the room look half its actual size. It smelled like mouse poop and mothballs.

Right in the center of the room, Christopher sat tied to what looked, at first glance, like a giant black and crooked finger with thin spikes off the tip. Then Weston realized it was an abstract cast-iron sculpture, only four feet tall, but probably heavy as hell. Christopher sat on the floor in front of it with his legs straight out, rope wrapped around his torso and arms.

A red starburst stained the floor with Chris in the middle. For a heart-stopping second, Weston thought it was Christopher's blood. Then he saw the stain was dry. From his vision, Weston knew the mother and father had been murdered in the kitchen. So this must have been where LaFontaine had killed their little blond son.

A cold, oily sensation washed through Weston's gut. He belched up the taste of bacon, and could smell it on his breath. Weston didn't think he would ever eat another BLT in his life.

A single, incandescent bulb hung from the ceiling, casting a diffused yellow light over Christopher. He looked so small and vulnerable in the middle of the open floor. But scattered tracks in the dust ran from the doorway to where Christopher sat. So it looked like Chris had put up a good fight before they tied him up—not so vulnerable after all.

Which lifted Weston with a sense of pride.

I'm all right, but we have to hurry. Kate is suffering.

Weston hurried over and worked at the knots in the rope, a neat trick with the use of only one hand. As he had suspected, the sculpture didn't budge. He couldn't imagine how they had brought the thing upstairs, and then, after all that effort, left it in a dusty old room.

"You know what he's doing to her?" he asked as he dug his fingers into a triple-tied knot.

From behind the sculpture, he couldn't see Christopher's face. The boy didn't answer, except for a pained sigh.

Weston pulled loose one of the three knots. His fingers already ached. Damn, he wished he could use his other hand, but it hurt too much to move, and what movement he dared test didn't add up to much. The cut had probably severed some tendons. A quick thought—that he might never get full use of it again—tried to distract him. But losing a hand wouldn't mean a thing if he also lost Kate.

"Chris?"

It's my fault.

Weston grunted as he struggled to pinch his finger and thumb into the second knot. "That's crap. LaFontaine and his father are doing this. Mostly his father, from what I can gather."

But he's using me against her.

The knot gave way enough for Weston to squirm a finger in. The rope rubbed his cuticle raw, which started to bleed. Strangely, he couldn't feel it. His sawed wrist hoarded all his pain.

"Like he used Anna against me, and Lucy against you. But we can't blame *them*. So you can't blame yourself."

The second knot gave way. A cramp in his palm froze his fingers for a second. For Christ's sake, he couldn't even massage the cramp away unless he used his toes.

What she's seeing, I put in her head.

Weston shook his hand and warded off the cramp. He went at the last knot as hard as his fingers would let him. Chris felt guilty about what was happening to Kate, but it was Weston who had left her alone in that room, and was now taking too long to untie a damn rope.

"Forget it," Weston said. "None of this is on you. I wouldn't be here if it weren't for you. I was so stupid thinking the girls..." The sorrow over losing his family a second time mixed with his shame for letting the old man use them to get to him. The combination gave him the angry kick he needed to finish off the last knot.

He whipped the ropes away, which made a serpentine *hiss* as they rubbed against the sculpture.

Christopher wasted no time getting to his feet. Patches of dirt from the floor covered the backs of his legs. The seam under one sleeve of his hoodie was torn. Another sign that he had given LaFontaine hell while he tried to subdue the boy.

Then Weston realized that something didn't fit.

"Why did they tie you up?"

One corner of Christopher's mouth curled up.

To keep me from getting too close to them. I learned some of Jacques's tricks. Like blocking him from getting into my head.

Weston hadn't heard that name before, but he figured it belonged to the old man.

"That was you who put the vision of that girl in LaFontaine's head," Weston said. "You pulled on him what the old man's been pulling on us."

There came that swell of pride again. This kid never ceased to amaze him.

Christopher's smirk turned to a full grin. But it quickly turned to a frown.

Adrien was easy. But I think I can do it to Jacques, too.

Just not from here. And I can't do it alone.

Weston grunted. "That guy is cold as ice. You really think you can shake him up the same way?"

I got one glimpse into Jacques before he figured out what I was doing.

The thought turned Weston's stomach. He would not want to see what went on in that psycho's head.

Remember the woman in your sketch? I know who she is.

35

KATE STOOD AT THE MOUTH of the alley, wearing the Beast like he wore his security guard uniform.

This was her third time entering the alley. Apparently, Jacques LaFontaine planned on making her relive this moment over and over until...

What? Until he drove her crazy?

Because he was too old to wield a chainsaw and didn't have his lackey son to help finish the "meal?" Maybe he hoped he could kill her with mental torture.

Could that work?

As she strolled down the alley toward the Dumpsters, she felt woozy and sick, a lot like the first stage of a hangover. While she couldn't act on any of these sensations with her body not her own, she was perfectly able to *feel* it all. Fear, anger, guilt, pain, the uncontrollable urge to gouge her own eyes out. This all superimposed over the Beast's own sensations.

The cold breeze. The taste of garlic from his last meal. The sweat on his brow drying in the breeze. The giddy twitching low in his gut, like the nervous anticipation of an actor before taking the stage.

You, she thought, are a sick fuck.

The thought was for both the Beast and Old Man La-Fontaine. The Beast was just a memory, so she knew he couldn't hear her. But she hoped the old man could.

Again, Kate rode with Bonner as he came to her mother's lifeless body.

Next would come the knife.

And then the part that had never happened, but that the old man had cooked up just for her.

She thought his plan to kill her with insanity just might work.

"Hey, Mickey, what the hell is taking you so..."

What?

That was the other security guard's voice. Sure enough, when Bonner turned to the sound of the voice, his partner was coming down the alley, forcing him to quickly stow his knife out of sight.

What was the old man playing at?

Kate, the guard said, but his voice rang in her head, and he sounded like a young boy.

Kate, it's me.

A spark of hope fired within her. The voice belonged to Christopher.

I think I know how to fight Jacques. But I'm not strong enough to do it on my own.

Kate wanted to answer, but when she tried to project a thought, he didn't seem to hear her. And she knew the Beast's mouth wouldn't cooperate with her.

Noah is with me. We're in the room with you and Jacques.

But if we physically hurt him, I'm afraid we'll hurt you, too.

Figured. The old man seemed to have a trick at every turn. But Christopher thought he could fight him, and she had learned never to underestimate him.

Kate felt a pull, like a giant vacuum trying to suck her backward. Instead of getting whisked away, the Beast shuffled a few paces sideways, then turned back to her mother. He pulled his knife, ignoring the guard.

The old man had made a course correction.

But he hadn't yet pushed out Christopher. The boy could still speak to her.

His trick is to haunt people with the ones they love and lost. We have to do it to him.

Kate had a hard time believing such a wicked man could love anyone. He didn't even seem to love his son all that much. But that was on the surface. Because if he didn't, the old man wouldn't have thrown Kate into this nightmare to get revenge against her for shooting his son.

Bonner crouched down in front of Kate's mother and worked his fingers between her cold lips. Kate felt her mother's dry, sponge-like tongue as he gripped it.

Do you understand what you have to do?

She still couldn't answer him, but she did what she thought he wanted.

She let the old man's conjured nightmare continue to play out, so she could focus on sending him one of her own.

The Beast pulled out her mother's tongue.

36

TIME MUST HAVE HAD ABOUT as much weight in the old man's trap as it did in a dream.

Wasn't that basically what Kate was stuck in? A dream with Jacques LaFontaine at the controls of her subconscious. And like a dream, time stretched like taffy, curled, tied itself in knots, and left Kate with memories she never had time to make.

By rough count, the Beast—and Kate—had now assaulted her mother's body at least eighteen times. Eighteen times in less than that many seconds. She would have thought she'd be desensitized to seeing his brutality by now, and maybe she would be if *seeing* was all she had to do.

Immersed in all of the Beast's senses, the experience felt too real to get used to. Every time he cut her mother, a shudder rumbled through Kate's soul, a soul that was barely intact.

Her only comfort came from the image she sculpted in her

mind's eye. A little scenario that she could feel Christopher and Noah both helping to shape. Something in their joint minds that, once complete, they could send roaring into the old man's mind.

That was the theory, at least.

So while she had to suffer through the horrifying loop of her mother's mutilation—and, Christ, did she suffer—every other resource of her psyche went toward their last chance to strike back at the old man.

And she had little doubt this *was* their last chance. Because if they actually managed to get inside his head, but the plan backfired, all three of them would probably find themselves in a rubber room.

Or a coffin.

37

WESTON STOOD IN THE LITTLE boy's bedroom, holding Christopher's hand while Christopher hung onto Kate's— though she showed no sign that she was aware of his touch. Weston's body stood in the room, but his mind had gone to what he came to call Christopher's psychic graveyard.

This graveyard didn't have any tombstones or crypts. What it did have was an enormous collection of fragments the boy had gathered from the places where tragedy lingered. Not images, or sounds, or any kind of physical sensations. More like an ocean littered with raw emotion.

According to Christopher, these gathered pieces could work to fuel the spectacle they had constructed for La-Fontaine's father, the same way the old man used the emotional suffering of his victims to feed his own power. But Christopher had come by these fragments honestly, collecting them after the suffering had ended, in order to *help* not harm.

As grim as it sounded, if Christopher had to carry the emotions of the dead in a psychic graveyard, he had every right to raise those dead and ask them to earn their keep.

Are you ready, Noah?

"Yes," he replied, hearing his voice buzz in his skull as if he spoke with his ears plugged. "What about Kate?"

She'll be ready.

"How will she know we've started?"

She'll know.

38

HALFWAY DOWN ANOTHER TRIP INTO the alley, the Beast came to a halt, his shoes scuffing the grit on the concrete.

The hesitation told Kate what she needed to know.

The battle had begun.

Balling up every emotion she had, including the overwhelming flood of other emotions crashing through her from some unknown force, she concentrated on pushing what had started in her, Weston, and Christopher's minds into the old man. Part force of will, part letting go of all control.

Then she felt herself falling. Falling out of the Beast's body, through the ground, into a washed out infinity of gray that slowly darkened the deeper she fell. Her stomach did a dizzy twirl.

A few seconds passed, maybe not even, before she hit bottom, a new world rising up around her.

The boy's bedroom back at the house. Her surroundings blazed with stunning detail. Right down to the dust on the radio controlled monster truck, to the browned edges of the Tigers pennant, to the electric taste in the air and its static pull on the hairs on her arms. But none of it was real. This was a dream.

Jacques LaFontaine's dream.

Kate stood with Weston and Christopher, their hands linked like a chain.

Facing them—the old man. He no longer held his hands out. His arms were relaxed at his sides. He had a bewildered look on his face, exaggerated by his shriveled features. His eyes looked as if they could roll right out of his head. His lips had shrunken into wrinkled flaps of skin that left his now toothless and gray gums exposed.

He looked *older* than ninety now. Much older. Their combined psychic energy not only stripping away what power he'd gained tonight, but for the last hundred fifty or so years.

A thin sigh came out his ruined mouth as if he were deflating.

Christopher lifted his chin. If the boy had been able to see, he'd be looking down his nose at the old man.

Hello, Jacques.

Another deflating sigh. Without a full set of lips, Kate didn't think he'd be able to talk. But dreams didn't care about physical defects.

"How..." The corners of his eyes wrinkled as if he wanted to narrow them, but couldn't. "You can't. You won't."

Kate sneered. "We already have, asshole."

The corners of his mouth curled up. His non-lips spread apart like a gaping wound. "You're in my mind. So you play by my rules."

A hand rested on Kate's shoulder. The hand smelled of rot. She turned to look. It was a delicate hand, skin black and torn, exposing bone. Maggots writhed between the fingers.

"Why did you cut out my tongue, Kate?" her mother said.

Kate could feel her mother's breath on her neck. It smelled like the inside of a crypt.

The maggots wriggled their way across Kate's shoulder and under her shirt collar. It became difficult to tell the difference between her crawling skin and the crawling larvae. But she gritted her teeth and turned her gaze back on the old man.

"You idiot," she said. "You're messing with the wrong person."

A bump where his eyebrow used to be lifted, stretching the frail skin of his eyelid. "I'm glad the storm didn't kill you. I love your feisty but empty threats."

Kate laughed. "That wasn't a threat. That was information."

As if they'd rehearsed this moment, Christopher took her words as a cue. He released his grip on their hands and stepped forward.

Do I scare you, Jacques?

The old man scoffed. "Not hardly."

Your mistake.

Now the old man's son stood up. Blood soaked the front of Adrien LaFontaine's shirt so thoroughly, it shone in the light like the surface of a still pond.

"I'm dying, Dad. I'm dying, and you're wasting your time *playing* in their heads."

"I'm doing this for you, you ungrateful nag." The old man raised a hand to his mouth, fingers like spindles. He shook his head. "You're on the floor. You're already dead."

His wide eyes snapped to Christopher. "Do you think I can't recognize my own methods? I've been doing this more than a century longer than you, *boy*."

LaFontaine moved to his father's side, took him by the

elbow. "He's stronger than you think. You know that."

"He isn't as strong as me."

You're right. I'm not.

Christopher looked at Weston, then looked to Kate, then back to the old man. Kate could feel the energy pulsing through the boy. Each pulse had a different flavor. Anger. Terror. Grief. Loneliness. But they weren't his emotions. They belonged to the souls it was his burden to carry.

But we *are.*

"Sentimental claptrap." The old man tugged his arm away from his son. "I'll give you credit for your effort. But it changes nothing."

Movement on the other side of the bed drew Kate's attention.

A little girl with Down syndrome, about Christopher's age, stared across the room at the boy.

Lucy.

For a second, Kate didn't understand why she could see her. Before, they hadn't been able to see each other's illusions. Then she remembered where she was. Like the old man had said—his head, his rules.

"Chris," Lucy said, voice soft and full of caring. "You have to stop. Don't you want to find me?"

Kate wanted to scream for Christopher not to listen, to remind him that this Lucy was a lie. But she wouldn't insult the boy. He didn't need reminding.

I love my Lucy. But you are not *Lucy.*

The old man hooked a thumb at LaFontaine. "And this isn't my son. Are we done?"

"Dad," LaFontaine said with all the gentle care of a loving son. "We're nowhere near done."

The old man waved LaFontaine away and staggered sideways to put distance between them. His legs, so thin now that his herring bone pants swayed like the clothes of a scarecrow that had lost its stuffing, betrayed him. He tripped. But managed to shift his slight weight so he fell to a sitting position on the edge of the bed. The creaking from the bed springs just as easily could have come from the old man's joints in his condition.

He was so frail. So vulnerable. Why couldn't Kate jump him, wrap her hands around his droopy jowled neck, and snap it like a dead tree stalk? If she killed him in a dream, couldn't that kill him for real?

Christopher must have picked up what she was thinking. He turned and shook his head. His calm and concentrated expression convinced her that he could take care of this. She had to trust that.

Her musing had distracted her. She became aware of her mother's rotting hand still on her shoulder, and the legion of maggots dropping down her shirt like grains of rice.

The old man glared at his son. His gaze hesitated on the ragged bullet hole in LaFontaine's chest. Blood continued to gush in rhythmic spouts out of the wound. An exaggeration fit for a nightmare.

"You never loved me," LaFontaine said.

That pulled the old man's gaze the rest of the way to his son's face. The skin around his mouth puckered in what he probably meant as a sneer, though it could have been a smile. "If I didn't love you, I would have eaten you a long time ago."

LaFontaine's eyes flashed. "But you were going to, weren't you? The only reason you've kept me around is to use me to do the slaughtering so you don't have to get your hands bloody anymore."

"If I didn't love you, then why is that boy making you argue with me?" He turned to Christopher. "You'll have to do better than this."

Lucy came around the bed. She stepped right up to Christopher and put her hands on his cheeks. An illusion, yes, but maybe not to Chris.

"I don't have to be real," she said, and he went rigid, but didn't flinch away. Not even when she kissed him.

The old man did his sneer/smile. A jerky breath popped from his mouth. His best attempt at a laugh.

"How does it feel to have her touch you?" He stood, steady on his feet now. Some of the wrinkles on his face smoothed. He was getting to Christopher, and feeding on his emotions.

"Now," he said with a gleeful creak in his voice. "How would you like to *see* her?"

39

WESTON HAD NO DOUBT THE old man could do it, and the idea chilled him deeper than any blizzard could. Tricking Christopher into thinking he could see by forcing images into his mind as clearly as if real? Weston couldn't begin to guess the effect that would have on the boy's psyche.

They had to stop this now.

"Chris, time for part two."

The old man turned at the sound of Weston's voice. Enough skin had returned around his eyes that he could squint. A canine tooth as polished as porcelain pushed its way out of his gums. He seemed to be regenerating awfully fast. Perhaps a testament to Christopher's psychic potency.

Weston's gut clenched. He had the sudden certainty the old man would win. He would break them down. Then, maybe the real LaFontaine—who was still alive last time Weston checked—would struggle to his feet and hack them to pieces.

Christopher's lips parted. His breathing quickened. He closed his eyes and his eyes twitched under the lids as if in REM sleep, dreaming inside a dream.

Kate took Christopher's side, grasped his hand. "Don't let him do this to you."

Weston joined them and took Chris's other hand. "We're here. We'll give you all the strength we have."

Christopher's head shook in small jags like a nervous tic. He inhaled deeply through his nose.

Lucy, her hands still on his face, smiled.

I can smell her. It's the soap they gave us at the home.

"Fight, Chris," Weston said. He could smell the soap, too. Even though he'd never before smelled it himself. "You have our strength. Take it."

The boy's sharp gasp told Weston they were too late. And as a smile blossomed on Christopher's face, a dark pit opened in the center of Weston's soul.

The old man had his claws in the boy.

They had lost.

She's beautiful. Oh, God, Noah. She's beautiful.

Weston hung his head. Tears blurred his vision.

"No," Kate pushed through clenched teeth. "No."

The old man laughed. His lips closed in as more teeth grew behind them. His grin took on a normal curve, but it looked just as ugly as it had without lips.

"She's beautiful." He clapped his hands together and held them against his chest. "Isn't that just the sweetest thing?"

Christopher cried. His tears collected on Lucy's hands.

"Stop it," Weston shouted, spraying spittle. "He's just a boy. And you're *devastating* him."

The old man shook his head. "Wrong and wrong. We both know he's not *just* a boy. And the young man's smile and tears of joy hardly speak to any destruction. Quite the opposite. I have raised him up."

"Only to let him fall and break," Kate said.

He shrugged. His shoulders carried more meat now, covering the bones that had once pushed out against his thin skin. "At least he will have tasted true happiness before his inevitable descent."

Weston let go of Christopher's hand and charged forward to knock the old man's new teeth out of his new mouth, but someone gripped his elbow and held him back.

He turned.

Christopher had his arm. Lucy was gone.

It's okay, Noah. He forgot that emotions can feed me, too.

The boy stepped forward until only a couple feet separated him from the old man. Christopher's blind gaze aimed over the old man's head as if the old man wasn't even there.

I can thank you twice. Once for giving me a chance to see how beautiful Lucy is. And once for giving me the chance to use that memory to make me stronger than you.

The old man, who looked as if he had regained everything he'd lost in the last few moments, rose to his feet. He stood nearly two feet taller than the boy. By standing, he closed the small distance between them.

For a moment, he could have been a proud grandfather looking down at his grandson. But the old man's crooked grin and dark eyes stopped the comparison dead.

"Stronger than me?" He leaned forward, putting his face only inches from the boy's. "Haven't you been paying attention?"

Yeah. And you've taught me a whole bunch of good stuff.

Christopher backed away until he once again stood between Weston and Kate. He nodded.

Okay, Noah. Time for part two.

40

KATE DIDN'T KNOW WHAT "PART TWO" meant. Obviously it was something Weston and Christopher had come up with while she had been trapped in her looping nightmare. It bothered her a little that she wasn't in on it. All her focus had been on building an illusion of LaFontaine to guilt-trip his father.

Then Christopher's voice came into her mind.

I'm sorry, Kate. Jacques was in your head. We couldn't risk him knowing what we really had planned. Creating his son was just a distraction.

It wasn't fair to them, but Kate still felt a little bent out of shape for being left out. She understood, though. And Christopher was right. The old man had put all of his attention on infiltrating her mind and spreading misery. Which had given Weston and Christopher a chance to conspire.

But what could they possibly have in mind?

The old man opened his mouth as if he meant to ask the

same question. Then he clamped it shut as the boy's bedroom fell apart like a cheap movie backdrop. The ceiling crumbled to pieces that fluttered away in a breeze like scraps of paper. Warm sunlight poured in from above. The walls fell outward, exposing an open wheat field, and when they hit the ground, they exploded into dust that the breeze carried away as well.

The open air and the noon sun felt glorious. Kate tipped her head back, closed her eyes, and reveled in the dry heat. The whisper of wheat stalks bending in the wind provided a soothing white noise. For an instant, Kate forgot all about the old man, LaFontaine, the house, the Beast. All of that fell apart and blew away just like the bedroom had.

Until the old man shrieked.

Kate's eyes snapped open. The chill that ran through her killed the feel of the sun on her skin. His shriek had sounded inhuman, and twisted with blatant angst.

He fell to his knees. The wheat stalks obscured him from the shoulders down. He threw his head back, but not for the sunlight. He bayed like a lamb to slaughter.

"You can't," he cried. Then he looked pleadingly at the conjured image of his son who had followed them to this new dreamscape. "Don't let them do this."

Adrien LaFontaine lowered his head, reached down and put a hand on his father's shoulder. "You brought this on yourself. You and the house brought them here. It was only a matter of time before you met your match."

The old man swung an arm and knocked away his son's hand. He stood up and gave LaFontaine the most furious glare Kate thought she'd ever seen. "How do they know?"

His son didn't respond.

Kate glanced at Christopher and Weston. They stood in the same relative position from her as they had in the bedroom.

The only thing that had changed was the scenery. Both of them kept their attention fixed on the old man, stares intense. Christopher swayed gently like another stalk of wheat. He had that look he sometimes got, where it seemed as if he could see, while at the same time oblivious to his surroundings.

She also saw something different in him, too. It could have been her imagination, goaded by the unusual circumstances. But she swore he carried a new and rigid strength, as if he had crossed some threshold to a higher level of self-confidence, of maturity.

Then he said to the old man, *Adrien isn't your slave anymore.*

The old man slowly turned, eyes shifting back and forth, unable to keep them still. "This thing you conjured up isn't my son. You think I don't know that? You think Adrien—the *real* Adrien—is your friend?"

Christopher shook his head.

He's a monster, like you. He's just not as much *of a monster.*

"Bah." The old man swatted the air with his hand. He pivoted in a circle, scanning the horizon, until he came to a stop, his back to them, facing a small brick house about five acres away. The wheat field stretched nearly all the way to the house, but stopped before a quartet of apple trees in the house's yard.

Kate crept in a shallow arc so she could see the old man's face.

The rims of his eyes were red and moist. One hand trembled at his side, his fingers twitching as if he wanted to grab hold of something but couldn't bring himself to do it.

"It's just a little farther," he whispered, only slightly louder than the hush through the wheat. "Just a little."

The pollen in the air made Kate's nose itch. The itch was something far away, though. She couldn't get over the haunted look on the old man's face. She recognized that look. It was the same devastated expression she saw when she had to tell next of kin that they had lost a loved one.

Somehow, Christopher and Weston had figured out the one person who could haunt Jacques LaFontaine.

But where was this person?

"A little farther," he said again.

His son said, "You'll never make it, Dad. You never did."

Then the old man looked down at his feet. His face crumbled and he broke into thick sobs from deep down in his throat.

Kate could just make out a form in the wheat before him. She could tell it was a person, but not much more than that.

The strength the old man had regained from Christopher began to melt away again. A youthful ninety became a hundred, then a hundred twenty. His jowls sagged. His face thinned and wrinkled. His shoulders hunched forward.

He didn't appear to notice the changes. The figure laying at his feet commanded his full attention.

The old man knelt, the wheat spreading around him.

Kate moved in closer. Her curiosity wouldn't let her do anything else. But she started to a halt when a baby's cry cut the silence.

"Stop it," the old man growled. "Damn you. Stop this."

He knew all too well that what he saw wasn't real, but it didn't matter. As Kate could attest to, knowing the lie didn't make it any easier to bear when presented in such encompassing detail.

He reached down and lifted a naked and bloody baby boy, the umbilical cord still attached to his belly. He tucked the infant against his side like a football, then pulled a pocket knife and unfolded the blade.

Kate's every nerve sparked. Was this man really so cruel that he would murder a defenseless baby?

But the old man didn't use the knife on the baby. He used it to cut the umbilical cord.

Breath shaky, Kate continued her path forward until the woman in the wheat came into view. She lay on her back, her cotton dress hiked up to her thighs and bloody down the front. Her legs were bent and turned to one side with her knees together. A bloody, wet glop, with half of the umbilical cord attached, weighed down a patch of wheat stalks behind her legs.

Instead of holding her newborn to her breast or cooing in his ear, she lay still, eyes open and staring at nothing, jaw slack, skin as white as snow.

The old man put away his knife and held the baby out in front of him as if he meant to pass it to someone. He shook his head and cried. The bones in his arms began to show prominently against his loose skin.

LaFontaine stuck his hands in his pockets and stepped through the wheat until he looked down over his father's shoulder.

"That was the day you found out," he said. "When you tasted the power of her misery as she struggled to give birth to me and then bled to death."

The old man's arms trembled. The baby was too heavy for his deteriorating muscles. Even though she knew it wasn't real, Kate hurried over and took the baby from him, wrapped the infant in her arms. The warmth of his tiny body as he nuzzled against Kate's chest made her eyes water. None of this was real. Not the field, the sun, the wind, the smell of birth. This baby. None of it.

Yet it still broke Kate's heart.

Not for the old man. Especially if what LaFontaine said was true—that his father had learned his taste for suffering from the death of his own wife in childbirth.

"Did you feed a little on me, too?" LaFontaine asked. "Did the terror of a baby's sudden pull from the womb add another hour or two to your life?"

The old man covered his face with his hands and dragged them down, smearing blood from forehead to jaw.

"I didn't do it on purpose. I didn't know it would happen. Besides, she…" He trailed off and looked skyward.

"She was going to die anyway," LaFontaine said. "Is that what you were going to say?"

A gust of wind blew through, shaking the wheat, and carrying with it a winter chill. Kate thought she could smell ice.

The old man tried to stand, but he didn't have the strength to get up on his own. He dropped back to his knees. Tears dyed red with blood dripped off the tip of his nose. Yellow snot collected on his thin upper lip.

His gaze traveled from his son, to Weston and Christopher, then over to Kate and the baby wriggling in her arms. Then the old man's eyes looked down at the placenta. He opened and closed his mouth as if he wanted to say something, but couldn't think what.

"All those years of merely draining your victims of their psychic energy until they were dead was *nothing* after this," LaFontaine said. "Not when you felt the bliss of my mother's pain and knew that butchering people at the height of their suffering would give you so much more. Your victims not only kept you younger, they made you stronger. More powerful. And then, when your son was old enough, you demanded he help, threatening to *eat* him if he didn't obey."

Kate hugged the baby tighter. "This is so sick."

The old man once more gazed across the field to the house. "I tried to get her home. I tried."

"These people won't offer forgiveness, Dad." LaFontaine bent at the knee and spoke directly into his father's ear. "No one will."

A tremor shook the old man's entire body. His mouth opened so wide, Kate could see the dark hole of his throat. And when he screamed, the dream shattered around them.

They were back at the house, in the little boy's bedroom.

Kate knelt on the floor, her arms cradling an empty space.

Christopher released a strained sigh and his legs gave out. Weston caught the boy and held him up.

The old man dropped onto his side and curled into a fetal position, the irony not lost on Kate. He pressed his wet face against the carpet and gently shook as he sobbed.

The imaginary Adrien LaFontaine was also gone.

The real one still lay on the floor to one side of Kate, but he had rolled onto his back.

And he had Kate's gun.

41

KATE FROZE. HER EYES LOCKED on the gun.

He held it against his bloody chest, not aiming it at anything. He lifted his head to regard Kate.

"Aw, shit," Weston said. His voice sounded distant.

A trickle of Kate's remaining adrenaline made her rapid pulse loud in her ear. Her muscles coiled. She was ready to pounce.

LaFontaine must have seen it. He raised the gun, aimed it at her. "Wait."

"What's the point?" Kate asked. "You're nearly dead. It's over."

"I need..." He winced. Coughed. Blood flecked his chin. Kate then noticed the wheeze coming through the wound in his chest. She must have hit a lung when she shot him. "...I need to thank the boy."

Kate spat air. "Thank him for what?"

"He's amazing." He cocked his head, trying to see

Christopher.

Kate was tempted to take the chance to tackle him, but a finger twitch was all it would take for him to give her a matching bullet hole.

"Do you hear me, Christopher?" LaFontaine asked. "They have no idea."

Christopher showed no sign that he heard. Weston had managed to get him steady on his feet, but his head leaned to one side and he rocked while Weston kept his arm across the boy's shoulders. His sightless eyes stared at someplace beyond this room. He had retreated into the haze.

LaFontaine looked back to Kate. "You have no idea."

Then he swung his arm, bringing the gun around so it aimed at his father, and pulled the trigger.

The old man's skull blew open, spreading gray matter, blood, and bone chips across the carpet.

Kate started. The gunshot set her ears ringing. The smell of gunpowder filled the room.

LaFontaine dropped the gun and leaned his head back.

He stared at the ceiling, smiling.

Not even the blood on his teeth could dull their signature shine.

EPILOGUE

"What it lies in our power to do, it lies in our power not to do."

~*Aristotle*

42

TWO WEEKS LATER, KATE LEANED against the Rambler while she waited for the gas pump to finish filling it up. The Arizona sun made the metal hot to the touch. But Kate could handle hot. It would probably take another month before she felt completely thawed out from their time in Coolidge Township.

A black Ford F-150 on the other side of Kate's pump rumbled to life and pulled away, giving her a clear view of the station. She could see Weston through the window of the mini-mart as he called out the options from the snack rack, Christopher at his side.

Sometimes Chris went with Funyuns. She hoped to God he didn't this time. The smell seemed to take days to come out of the wagon's upholstery.

Christopher stood still, his face turned down as he listened to Weston. Kate watched him. Every time she did, she expected to see what she had always seen before the night at the Stoker house—a precocious young boy with a gift she didn't fully understand, except that it connected the three of them like she never imagined she could connect with anyone.

She still saw the quiet intelligence in the boy. Still felt the bond of his gift. But those things didn't seem as important anymore. They were background details. Because now she saw an untapped strength. His was no longer a gift she didn't understand. It was a power she could not comprehend.

She had grown complacent. She had thought she knew what to expect from him, however strange it sometimes seemed. Then they had met Jacques LaFontaine. Someone with abilities similar to Christopher's, but magnified a hundred times. They never stood a chance against him. They should have died in that house. But they hadn't. As it turned out, Kate had not only underestimated the old man, she had grossly underestimated the boy.

LaFontaine's last words rang over and over in her head.

You have no idea.

He was right. She didn't. She wondered if she ever would.

One thing was for sure, she wouldn't let herself get complacent again. That was a mistake none of them could afford. Especially considering the reason behind their travels across the country in the first place.

The Beast.

If an old man in the middle of nowhere could pose such a threat, what might they find if they finally reached their goal?

Kate must have zoned out. Weston and Christopher were halfway back to the Rambler, and she never saw them come out of the mini-mart.

Squinting in the sun, Weston looked at her as he approached. He turned his mouth down. When he reached her, he asked, "Everything all right?"

She didn't answer.

Weston nodded. "Yeah."

They got back in the Rambler, Weston behind the wheel.

Kate heard the crinkling of a plastic bag behind her as Christopher tore open his snack. A second later she caught a whiff of Funyuns. She groaned and leaned back against the headrest. "Chris, really?"

Weston smirked as he started the engine. "I told him you wouldn't approve."

"They're so gross," she said, and laughed. It felt good after all that heavy thinking. "I don't know how you can eat those things."

Christopher crunched his way through one.

I like *Funyuns*.

This from the kid who had won a psychic war against a two hundred-year-old mad man. But it reminded Kate of an important truth she had let herself forget. Power or no power, he was still an eleven-year-old boy.

He was still Christopher.

We hope you enjoyed this book, and if you did, we'd greatly appreciate a quick review on Amazon, Goodreads and other review sites. And be sure to tell your friends about the book as well. Reader recommendations go a long way toward spreading the word about a good book.

If you have any questions about the Linger Series or any of our other books, feel free to contact us at *BraunHausMedia.com*

Thank you.

Robert Gregory Browne
Editorial Director
Braun Haus Media, LLC